I0571543

Bloody October

A collection of chilling tales inspired by the
haunted season.

Edited by
Christopher Allan Death

Fort Collins, Colorado

This anthology is a work of fiction. All names, characters, places, and incidents either are products of the authors' imaginations or are used fictitiously. Any resemblance to actual events or locales or persons, living or dead, is entirely coincidental.

All stories are copyright of their respective authors.

Text set in Times New Roman.
Title text set in Tooth Ache.

ISBN-13: 978-0-6152-2245-5

Cover art by Steve Cartwright

Table of Contents

October's Gift
by Christopher Fulbright

Previously published in Whispers from the Shattered Forum

It wasn't so much that Leonard wanted to die, he just didn't want to live anymore. He couldn't face one more day jam-packed with one non-event after another. One more day of walking by the phone, angry because it refused to ring. One more day of hollow yearning and masturbation that did nothing but raise his awareness of how empty the house was and probably always would be.

It would be best, he figured, if one morning -- one morning soon -- he just kept on sleeping and never woke up.

He stared out the window at rain that showered his small lawn. His cat, Lucy, hopped up into the window sill and nudged his hand. He felt her tongue like a small strip of sandpaper along one finger and stroked her shiny black fur. She looked up at him and meowed; the only faithful female in his life, and she was a feline.

No, he didn't want this anymore.

He didn't want the mortgage, car payments, or the water, phone, and electric bills. He didn't want to scour local bars or Colfax Avenue for a night's companionship. He didn't want to sleep, shit, shower, shave, or watch anymore crappy daytime television. The house was closing in on him. Depression deepened and became a murk through which he groped half-blind, day after miserable fucking day.

Joy, he thought cynically. *Joy comes in the morning.*

Another time, the rain would have been the perfect opportunity to sit and write. He used to think he wrote his best poetry on days like this, the weight of depression crushing his life. That was when the real stuff came out, the stuff that people wanted to read. Because people were sick like that. They wanted to see your suffering.

Leonard gave Lucy a pat as she lay in the window sill.

He turned away and moped back down the hall to the bathroom.

He gazed at his own whiskery face in the mirror and touched his cheek. Was he unattractive? Whatever happened to that old doormat saying: It's what's inside that counts?

Maybe that's the problem, he thought.

As if detached from the rest of his body, his hand moved down to the counter and pinched a fresh, unused razor between forefinger and thumb. His left hand turned palm up, baring the underneath side of his wrist. The blade was sharp. It pricked through instantly, close to the vein.

One hard slice and a short wait. That's all. Just sit on the toilet (a fitting place to end it) and watch the final moments of his life drip into sticky puddles at his feet.

He pushed harder. A bead of blood appeared, so did two others. He thought about how it might feel to cut himself open, to watch the skin part in the wake of the sharp blade. It was itching right now. He thought about scratching at the open wound. He imagined the blood surfacing to pour over his arm like magma boiling from a fault in the earth.

Can I do this? Do I really want to do this?

Leonard jerked the razor away from his wrist as if it were the fang of a venomous snake. The blade dropped into the sink and clinked around the drain. Turning on the water, he scrubbed the feeling of it from his skin. He splashed cool water onto his face.

"What am I doing?" He moaned. He leaned weakly over the wash basin. He breathed a deep, shuddering breath.

He could hear Lucy purring as she came down the hall. She stopped, stood at the threshold, and watched him.

Three weeks later, near the middle of October, Leonard packed his belongings, rented a U-Haul trailer, and finalized lease arrangements on his Denver home with a young couple from Scottsbluff, Nebraska. He grabbed Lucy, hopped in the car, took I-25 south, and never looked back.

Almost two hours later, they arrived in Woodland Park, a small mountain town west of Colorado Springs. They drove around for twenty more minutes before he and Lucy pulled to the top of a snow covered hill and fell in love.

They had a panoramic view from where they'd parked. Pikes Peak rose high and majestic to the south, Woodland Park itself surrounded on all sides by mountain ranges, resting in a lush bowl and valley. Snow blanketed the town for a quiet season of rest. Smoke plumed from chimneys like curls in the hair of Mother Nature.

They had parked in front of a house, not much bigger than a cottage really, and Leonard knew right away that this was where he needed to be. It wasn't big, but it didn't need to be big. Not exactly cheery, but it didn't need to be cheery either. Scrub oaks, blue spruce, and ponderosa pine filled the yard. Snow drifted around the trees and the porch. Mini-drifts of snow had gathered in the corners of the windows.

"What do you think Lucy?" He plucked the cat from the passenger seat and propped her up at the window. She put her paws on the door and stood on hind legs.

"Meow," Lucy said.

Smiling, Leonard reached into the glove box to pull out his notebook and a pen. He tore off the first page of addresses and copied information off the real estate sign at the corner.

As he scribbled, Lucy began to growl.

He looked over. She was upright against the passenger side window. Her hackles went up, fur bristling. She hissed like a tiny panther and swiped her paw at the glass, claws screeching.

Beyond the dark cottage windows was an old woman's head. Her hair was long and gray, face puckered with age. Her eyes were staring black pits. Wormy lips curled into a rot-toothed grin.

Invisible fingers of ice walked Leonard's spine. His high spirits broke like cold glass, shattered by the touch of fear.

"Lucy," he whispered urgently. "Stop it!"

The woman -- rather, the woman's head -- stayed at the window. Surely she had a body...he just couldn't see it. Too dark in there, he thought, the windows are frosted.

She watched him.

He reached quickly down into the seat to snatch Lucy from her position. The screeching of her claws was too much. She hissed when he touched her. She scratched him and drew blood.

"Shit!"

Lucy's hair stood on end. She hopped back to her position and growled deep in her throat.

Leonard started the car and pulled slowly away. He resisted the urge to look back over his shoulder. He knew she'd still be there. Watching them.

Woodland Park wasn't big, but a newcomer could still get turned around on all the slushy back roads, which is exactly what he did.

Eventually, he made his way back to the main highway.

They cruised up and down the main strip a couple of times before they spotted the real estate offices that shared a building with the Gold Mine Café. An "OPEN, PLEASE COME IN" sign hung in the front window. The parking lot shone with ice as he turned in and parked next to a long blue Cadillac. Steps led up to a small front porch, icicles hanging from the eaves.

Leonard mounted the salt-speckled stairs and was about to reach for the doorknob when a well-fed man with a big smile opened the door for him.

"Well, hi there!" He waved Leonard inside, closing the door on harsh winds that kicked up. The man peeked outside. New flurries fell from the sky. "You're just in time! I was closin' up shop when I saw you pull in. Like some coffee? Still hot."

"No thanks. Actually, I was coming to ask about the house up on——" he paused to check his notes, "Park Street? We were driving by——"

"You and the wife?"

"No wife," Leonard said soberly. "Me and my cat."

The fella nodded. He knew exactly which house Leonard was talking about. They discussed the floor plan. The man, Benny, drew him a rough sketch of the layout of the place. Told him there were washer and dryer hookups, but no washer and dryer. One bedroom, one bath, one living room, and a small entryway that might be called a foyer—which the man pronounced foy-yay, like he was French. Leonard thought everything sounded great.

"When could I move in?" he asked.

"Move in?" Benny said, surprised. "Don't you want to take a look inside?"

Leonard shrugged. "We snooped around a little bit today -- it looks perfect, and it's just the right price."

Benny sighed and looked resigned. "Well, okay. You'll have to fill out an application. There'll be a $25 fee for that and, of course, you'll have to wait for that to clear before you move anything in."

"Fine, I can stay in one of the hotels down the highway."

"The Grand View is nice. And they allow pets."

"Great."

Benny reached into a desk drawer and gave Leonard an application and a pen. While Leonard filled out the application, Benny looked suspiciously out at Leonard's car with the U-Haul trailer hitched on back.

"Say," Benny said, "is everything okay with you...I mean, I don't want to pry but..."

Leonard looked up from the application, amused. "But you're going to anyway?"

"Seems like you're runnin' from something. And...doin' all this without even seeing the cabin. It's not all that spectacular a place, you know."

"One man's trash is another man's treasure," Leonard said, filling out the last few lines and signing his name to the application. He gave Benny $25 cash. "And I'm always this nervous when I'm running from myself."

Benny looked at him to see if he was serious, wasn't quite sure, and decided to drop it. He shrugged. "Okay, well. This ought to take a couple of days -- 24 hours at least. You want to give us a call when you get settled..."

Leonard stood up. "I'll call as soon as I find a room and give you the number where I'm staying."

"Okay," Benny stood up and extended his hand. "Well, I guess that's it. We should be in touch."

"Great. Thanks for your help."

"Anytime."

Leonard headed for the door, pushed it part of the way open, and paused when the cold wind curled in around him.

"Somethin' else?" Benny asked.

"Well, I'm just curious. We were up looking at the place today, and there was an old woman inside -- seemed kind of bothered that we were snooping around. She moving out soon?"

"Old woman?" Benny blinked.

"Yeah, long gray-black hair. 'Bout sixty maybe...couldn't really tell from where I was parked."

Benny looked Leonard carefully up and down. "The last old lady who lived in that house died two years ago."

Leonard and Lucy were on their second day staying at the Grand View Motel when Benny from the real estate office called.

"Great news," he said. "It's all yours!"

Leonard met with him the next day, used the money from the sublet in Denver to pay cash for the deposit and first three month's rent, and moved in.

The cabin had been October's greatest gift to Leonard so far. He'd found some used furniture at one of the local Goodwill distributors and paid them to deliver. Nothing fancy; a couch, coffee table, old TV stand, and a television to go with it. The place came furnished with a queen-sized bed from one of the company's other rentals. He unpacked his clothes and typewriter, went shopping at the local City Market, and had everything he needed. His spirits were higher than ever. He almost forgot that, except for Lucy, he was completely and utterly alone.

Everything continued to be great -- he'd even gotten some new writing done -- until Halloween.

That night, Leonard lay on the couch watching television. Lucy lay on his chest, curled up and purring. All the lights were off. Blue shadows from the television flashed across the living room walls.

Earlier, as twilight deepened into night, he'd started a fire in the small fireplace. It crackled now with wicked orange flames. Beyond the fogged windows, he could see the blurred shape of a full moon.

That was when he thought of the old woman.

He hadn't thought of her since that first day, and now, seeing the blurred shape of the moon through the window, he remembered her piercing stare, her smile of rotted teeth.

...dead for two years...

Enough. He didn't believe in ghosts.

Then why am I afraid of them?

Because it's Halloween, he thought, that's why.

He lay there. He watched television, but didn't listen. Lucy purred on his chest. The fire popped again.

A crash sounded out on the porch.

Leonard jumped. Lucy darted off into the bedroom. He sat up and stared wide-eyed out the window.

It was just an icicle. Icicles will fall whenever they want to, he thought. Or maybe it was a Halloween prank, maybe some kids had thrown a snowball or -- why hadn't any children come to his door?

Oh God. Where are all the children?

His porch light didn't work, so he couldn't turn it on to let them know that they were welcome, but he had carved a Jack O' Lantern.

Maybe they know the house is haunted. Maybe they're afraid...

Or their parents wouldn't let them near the place, not knowing who might live here now, despite the Jack O' Lantern on the porch.

Leonard's skin crawled. Goosebumps rose along his arms and met at the back of his neck.

He sat up.

"Shit," he whispered.

He stood up and grabbed his jacket from the arm of the couch, not even venturing into the dark bedroom to look for Lucy. He convinced himself he was just going out for a minute. Just a minute -- up to the corner store. Or something.

Leonard slipped out the front door and slammed it behind him, instantly more at ease to be outside in the sobering cold air. Breath misted from his lips as he hurried to his car in the driveway.

His door was unlocked. He slid in quickly and slammed the door. He sat in the driver seat, regarding for a moment the carven features of the Jack O' Lantern flickering from his porch step. He realized he'd left the fire burning in the fireplace, but...

The windows were dark now. Not even light from the television.

He dug in his pockets, frantically looking for the keys, realizing: Lucy was in there. He had to go back in for her.

He probed for his keys. Where were those stupid keys?

Then he remembered. Inside on the kitchen table, right where he'd left them. His head fell with a defeated thud to the wheel.

He began to reason with himself. What was he really afraid of? Some old ghost story? Maybe the lights just couldn't be seen like this from out here...the way the night reflected in the glass. But he knew he should have been able to see the light from the television, at least.

He didn't see anything at all.

Just go in, grab the keys, and get the hell out of here.

He climbed back out of the car. He took careful steps back across the snowy lawn, feet crunching in icy drifts. He crept up the stairs. A blast of cold air penetrated his clothes. He stopped at the door and listened.

He couldn't hear anything inside. Not the television, not Lucy, not anything.

He wrapped his hand around the cold doorknob, turned it slowly, and pushed open the door.

Inside, the house was pitch black but for a few glowing embers in the fireplace. He could see nothing else. The door closed behind him.

He listened, and waited in silence.

Something shifted on the sofa.

Tentacles of fear constricted his heart. Why hadn't he remembered the damn keys? His mind raced, eyes trying to focus in the velvet darkness.

Footsteps, light and padded.

Something came near, something larger than a cat, and heavier. He could feel the floor shift beneath his own feet. He took a step back instinctively. The thing seemed to stop, breathing lightly.

Cool flesh touched his hand and he jerked away in terror. The thing found him again. It was another hand, small and frail.

An ember in the fireplace cracked. A flame sparked, catching the logs on fire again. As the flames grew, they slowly dissolved the veil of darkness.

A beautiful woman stood naked before him. Her long black hair shimmered. Her eyes closed as she came closer, her lips pursed and blood red.

"Don't be afraid," she whispered, taking his hands, guiding them. She leaned into a sensuous kiss.

He was terrified.

Her lips were warm, slightly damp, fitting the curve of his own lips. He relaxed and felt a stir in his groin. He opened his mouth slightly as they met in a second kiss, and her tongue probed against his, warm and inviting. She pulled him close. He could feel her breasts pressing against him. He took her into his arms and felt her heart beating rapidly, almost as if...almost as if she were...*purring*.

They came apart and she opened her eyes. They were the green, slitted eyes of a cat.

He couldn't breathe for a moment. Too startled. Impossible. How could she...what...? But the kiss. The silken feel of her skin. And suddenly, it didn't matter.

"Lucy?" He asked, trying a tentative smile.

She purred.

Heck Yeah
by Rob Rosen

Fred awoke with a start at the sound of a rustling noise outside his bedroom window. He checked the clock on his nightstand. It was four in the morning. A full moon hung low and bright in the otherwise pitch-black October sky, illuminating the entirety of his leaf-strewn backyard. He jumped up, opened the window, and craned his neck out. His dog, Chester, was frantically running in circles.

"What is it, boy? Is someone out there?" Chester rolled around on his back and whined. Not a good sign, not by a long shot. "Okay, I'm coming out," he said, loudly, more to scare off any unwanted visitors than to inform his dog.

With a baseball bat held firmly in hand, Fred walked into the backyard. Chester was now sniffing madly at the bushes abutting the house. Nervously, Fred approached the mutt, which yipped and growled, and then promptly peed on said bushes. "Hey," came a voice. "Now cut that out."

Both Fred and Chester backed up a few feet. "Wh...who's there? Come out before I start swinging," Fred shouted, and then raised his bat up high over his head.

"Hold your horses," replied the raspy voice. "I'm already wet. No need to get battered as well." And out stepped a strange man - strange, that is, not that he was where he was and when he was, but how he appeared. He was, from what Fred could see, ghastly pale, on the short side, exceedingly thin, and, weirdest of all, dressed in a style of clothing that Fred recognized as being outdated by a couple of hundred years, give or take a century.

"Who the hell are you?" Fred asked, with an equal amount of terror, anger, and curiosity; though, even without the bat, Fred knew for certain he could handle the odd, little man, if need be. Naturally, he prayed it wouldn't come to that.

"Name's Sam Waters. Pleased to make your acquaintance." There was something about the man's name that dimly lit a bulb in the recesses of Fred's addled brain, but he couldn't quite put his finger on why it sounded so familiar. Not yet, anyway. In any case, the bulb went suddenly dim when the man doffed his ancient cap and bowed ceremoniously. And that's when Fred spotted it. That is to say *didn't* spot it. For Sam was, much to Fred's dismay, quite scalpless beneath his hat.

"Holy cow," Fred gasped, and promptly sank to his knees. The bat dropped from his hand with a dull thud. "What the hell?"

"Actually," Sam said, with a snicker, as he approached the shocked Fred, "It's not Hell so much as Heck. And there ain't nothing holy about it."

"Huh?" was all Fred could manage to squeak out. Well, that and, "Put your damn hat back on, please."

"Ah, yes. Sorry, I forget that my appearance can be, um, *alarming* at times." A gross understatement, if ever Fred heard one. In the full light of the moon, and even without the whole scalpless thing, Sam was sickly pale, save for the numerous blue veins that coursed from his pitted forehead, down his sunken cheeks, and ended around his bony, hairless chin. And his teeth were crooked, jagged, and yellow enough to make even the most seasoned of dentists cringe. But it was his eyes, his eyes that glowed a sinister, hot, molten red, which caused Fred's heart to frantically skip a beat.

The fear most definitely showed in Fred's face. Chester too backed away, clearly sensing that all was not right with this grotesque picture.

"Now, now. I ain't gonna hurt either one of you," Sam said. "I was just searching for something when your dog cornered me in that there bush. He's a plumb good watchdog, he is." Which made Fred laugh, because Chester was the proverbial scaredy cat if ever there was one. Proof in point, he was cowering behind his master as Sam spoke, his shaking tail tucked neatly between his equally shaking legs. "Anyway," he continued, "seeing as I can't find what I'm looking for, I guess I'll be moseying along and let you get back to sleep, what with it being so late and all."

As he turned to go, Fred yelled, "Wait. Who and/or what are you? And what's this thing about Hell and Heck you mentioned?"

Obviously, it seemed way more sensible to let the scalpless man leave the backyard rather than call him back into it, but Fred's inquisitiveness got the better of him.

Sam stopped dead in his tracks and slowly turned to face his host. At that very moment the moon's rays hit Sam's ashen, pitted face and illuminated his ghoulish eyes, which then glowed and glimmered an even fierier red. Fred gasped but otherwise stood his ground. Chester, on the other hand, ran around the both of them and back inside the house.

"Smart dog," Sam commented.

"Why, am I in any danger?" Fred could barely get the words out.

"Not particularly. But you never now, right?" Sam flashed a wicked, crooked smile and then approached the now-leery Fred. "Anyway, you know that expression: the dead tell no tales? It ain't hardly true, not a lick. We got a boatload of 'em to tell. It's just we usually ain't got nobody to tell 'em to. But if you're interested…"

"Hold on," Fred said, almost in a whisper. "So you're…"

"Dead? As the proverbial doornail, my young friend. Been that way a long, long time now. Been this way just as long. Which is to say, un-dead. A demon, if you will. That's what you fellers been calling us for a while, anyways. Though, from what I hear, we ain't nothing like what you all think we are. Pretty much, we is the way we was when we was alive, only we ain't alive no more, if you get my meaning."

Fred hadn't a clue what the guy was talking about, and it had nothing to do with his appalling grammar. "So you're dead, but you ain't, er, *aren't* dead?"

"Sort of. I can't rest none until my soul is absolved. And that probably ain't never gonna happen." Sam frowned, which gave his freakishly hideous face an even more ominous appearance. Still, for some unexplainable reason, Fred felt sorry for the guy.

"And this Hell/Heck thing you mentioned before?" Fred asked.

"Ah, now that's the interesting thing. There's a Hell and a there's a Heaven, just like we was taught in church, even when I was a lad. But there's also a Heck. Hell's only for the really bad souls. Like them murderers, rapists, politicians, and such. Heck is for those people who the good Lord don't want but the Devil don't care to associate with neither. Seems we ain't evil enough for one place, nor good enough for the other. Though we sure got our fair share of that fire and brimstone stuff you hear about. Place stinks like a sulfur pit half the time and a clogged up toilet the other half."

"So Heck is kind of like limbo then, I take it?"

"Well, not exactly. Our souls aren't trapped, as you can plainly see."

"Plainly, yes. But isn't someone or something watching over you? To keep you down there, I mean."

"There is, yes. Or at least there was. From what I been told, it's kinda like Hell is a maximum-security prison and Heck a minimum one. They keep a more watchful eye on the worst prisoners, you see. Anyway, that's the way it's always been - until lately."

Fred didn't like the sound of that one. "You mean you guys are escaping?"

"From Heck? Yes. Or as you people say, heck yeah." Sam laughed at his ingenuity. "The Devil can keep an eye on his inmates. There ain't as many of them. The not-so-bad, however, outnumber the very bad fifty to one. Society, it would seem, ain't as civil a place as it once was, least when I was alive. So, from time to time, when the guards are too busy to notice, an inmate or two can sneak away; especially around Halloween, when the spirits are, well, more *spirited*. But we can only escape at night, like now. Demons don't like the daytime, you see. Your film directors got that one right. The sun burns us up like a real sonofabitch, it does."

Fred sat down on the cool ground, dumbfounded, and pondered what the creature was saying. It was, after all, a lot to take in. Sam too sat down, his ancient bones creaking and groaning as he did so; though the flames in his eyes still burned strong and bright. He was a nasty sight to behold, especially up close and personal like that. Luckily, he sat upwind from Fred, because the stench he emitted was nearly unbearable.

"But don't the guards get in trouble when one of you gets out?" Fred asked.

Sam paused and a mischievous grin spread across his nasty face. "Well now, if their boss finds out, I suppose they do. Though the one I got passed won't be gettin' into no trouble any time soon."

Fred gulped. "No? Did you have to kill him or something?"

"Can't kill the already dead, son. Nope, you gotta lop off their heads to get rid of 'em. That's the only way to keep them from getting back up again. No head, no brain, no guard. I done ate this one's. Didn't taste too bad, neither. Kind of like chicken, only greasier. And crunchier."

Fred wished he hadn't posed the question. Which is why he hesitated before asking, "If you don't mind telling, what happened to your, um, head?" Fred pointed to his own head and then winced.

Sam reached for his hat, but quickly remembered the effect that had, and kept it on. Instead, he scratched at it and replied, "Don't mind you asking one bit, young feller. It's kind of a curious thing, huh? It's not every day you run into a guy with no scalp."

"Thank God for that," Fred said, before he remembered his manners. "Oh, sorry."

"Don't be sorry. I know it's a fright to see. Fortunately, there ain't no mirrors in Heck. No God, neither. He stays darn clear. Guess he's busy doing whatever it is he does. Anyway, the scalp thing is what got me into Heck in the first place. You see…" Sam stopped in mid-sentence and the fire in his eyes dimmed at just that very moment. For the first time since they'd met, he looked frightened.

"What? What's wrong?" Fred asked, truly concerned for the strange, little man.

Sam pointed to the sky and then moaned. The sun had just started to rise above the horizon. Its light slowly began to reach the fog-chilled backyard, which caused Sam's already gruesome skin to smolder and sizzle. In an instant, the stench of burning flesh permeated the area around them. Fast as a whip, Fred ripped off the jacket he'd been wearing and covered Sam's head with it. "Go," he shouted. "Run, Sam. Run like…heck!"

"That's funny," Sam said, with a muffled chuckle. "I gotta remember that one." And with that, he was up and out of the backyard, though his putrid odor lingered for quite some time afterwards.

Fred sat and watched the sun come up. It felt warm and soothing on his own skin. "Poor Sam," he said as he walked back into his house, once the sunrise was over. "Poor, dead Sam."

But Sam was not really all that poor, nor, for that matter, all that dead. And Fred was soon to discover the reason for the lack of a scalp; though it didn't dawn on him until after he re-awoke later that day.

"Wait," he said over breakfast, snapping his fingers, as he sat at his kitchen table and downed his second cup of coffee. "Sam

Waters. I do know that name." Fred ran from the table, with Chester in hot pursuit, and found the document in his filing cabinet. It was the deed to his property, which also listed all the previous owners of the land his house rested upon. "There it is. Sam Waters. The original property owner in 1765. Well I'll be damn…er, a monkey's uncle."

Old Sam had finally returned home, Fred realized. But then a new thought popped into his head. "Or returned to the scene of the crime."

For the rest of that week, Fred chained Chester up in the backyard at night, dead certain the demon would return at some point. He didn't seem the type to give up all that easily. Fred was right, of course. On the following Saturday, he was roused by his dog's barks and growls. "Bingo," he said as he hopped out of bed, grabbing the pistol and the lighter from his nightstand; and then he ran out back. He tucked the gun in his back pocket, for safekeeping. "Sam, is that you?" he whispered into the chilly, night air.

"Sure as shootin'," came the response. "Sorry to disturb you."

"Yeah, well, I was expecting you."

Sam came out of the bushes he was once again rooting around in. His skin had healed some since the last time Fred had seen him, but he still looked frighteningly hideous, especially with the newly formed black scabs and purple bruises. "You was expecting me?" he asked.

"Yep," Fred replied. "I thought you might come looking for these." He took out a stack of ancient and yellowed papers from his jacket pocket.

"What you got there, young feller?" The fire in Sam's eyes leapt from his sockets and an evil, twisted sneer appeared on his withered face.

"You know what they are, but they're no longer where you left them, Sam."

"No? I buried them right next to the house. Right by that bush there, below the bedroom window. And deep, too, if memory serves me correctly."

"That you did, Sam, that you did. But the house isn't where it was when you first built it. It's been moved since then."

"Moved? How do you move a whole house?" Sam asked, edging in closer to Fred. Close enough for him to feel the heat from the demon's eyes. But with Chester chained at Fred's feet, Sam kept a respectable distance. Still, the young man could tell how desperate the demon was for the papers, but he had yet to figure out why.

"Oh, you can move a house easily enough. These days, anyway," Fred replied, quickly adding, "It's amazing what one finds under a house, huh, Sam?"

Sam tapped a bony finger on his pointed chin and laughed an evil, sinful laugh. "Damned if it ain't."

"Ah, the magic word - *damned*. I suppose digging up Indian burial grounds and then building a house on them is a definite no-no, right? Guess the Indians didn't like it too much either when they came back and found your house on top of their kin. Kind of explains the scalping thing, huh?"

Impatiently, Fred hissed, "They was plenty pissed, alright. Now give me back those papers so I can be on my way."

"But why would you need these sales receipts for the stuff you sold after you stole them from the Indians' graves?" Sam moved in dangerously close, causing Chester to jump up and snap at him. "Oh yes, I know what these are, Sam. They found them buried next to the house after they moved it. And the burial grounds, if you want to know, are now behind my fence, not inside of it. Only a fool builds his home on a graveyard, you know."

"Only a fool messes with the un-dead, young feller."

"And only a fool threatens someone who holds something of value of theirs. So back off, demon." Fred lit the lighter he had concealed in the palm of his hand and held its flame just below the stack of papers. Sam, as expected, backed away. "The only thing I want to know, Sam, is what do you think you'll gain by possessing them? Do you think that by destroying the evidence you can absolve your soul and go to Heaven? I doubt the Lord is that easily tricked."

A sinister smile again appeared on the dead man's face and the flames in his eyes flickered and then grew in intensity. Fred cringed and held the lighter even closer to the papers. "The Lord, as you say, ain't ever tricked. Not ever. But that's not who them papers is for. And Heaven ain't where I'm trying to get to."

"It ain't? I mean, *isn't*?"

"Nope. Heaven's an even more boring place than Heck. Hell is where all the action is. I mean to bring those papers to the Devil. To plead my case, so to speak. Now, if you don't mind, I'll take back what's rightfully mine."

"You're one evil sonofabitch, huh, Sam?"

"Evil as hell, young feller. Evil as hell." A frightful cackle erupted from the demon's twisted mouth. "Though them Injuns weren't any worse off when I stole their goodies out from under 'em. Was a lucky find when I stumbled across all them graves." Again Fred let loose with a hacking laugh, which was suddenly echoed by an even louder and surprising one from Fred.

"Well, today you're not so lucky, old timer. You can go to...*Heck*!" And with that, the lighter's fire reached the brittle papers and incinerated them in a flash of blinding, white light. "Anyway, I don't think my ancestors would approve."

Sam tilted his head, the flames in his eyes instantly turning black as coal. "What's that, Sonny?" he croaked, just before Fred lifted the gun out of his pocket and fired a blistering round right through the demon's neck. Sam's wretched head teetered and tottered in place before finally smashing to the ground, where it promptly exploded into a thousand dusty fragments of bone and gristle. His ancient body quickly, and thankfully, followed suit.

"You heard me," Fred said as he unchained his trusty dog and returned to his home. "And the name's not Sonny, it's Fred. Fred Eaglefeather. And the pleasure, I can assure you, was all mine."

The Farmer's Child
by Lawrence Dagstine

The ghost of Natalie Crosby was born on a farm one October night, the same month all ghosts of children are born. The farm's owner, Toby Linderscott, had captured her on a windy moonlit evening. Toby had gone to see her just at dusk while his wife of twenty years, Jackie, was running a bath for him, but he hadn't been able to stay long, and he'd gone to sleep with his flashlight, scared but proud of what he captured near the plowing fields. Still, if he felt brave enough, he intended to creep out after the others were asleep.

One of the nights he was awakened by a soft, urgent crying beside his bed, and found Natalie hovering beside his pillow and looking down at him. This was the first time she'd been to the house to look for him, the first time any of the children looked for him while, for three nights, he had been leaving her free to roam the cornhusks, the door of the barn open so that she could go in and out. Jackie was downstairs, up late as usual, working on her novel. His eldest son Brad, turning eighteen in a month, was often found conked out with his headphones on and the music blasting. Neither of them knew he collected the ghosts of children, and neither could see them or know the reason why.

Now he pulled the sheets over him hastily, folding it tightly against his chest with his arms, afraid that the spirit might be there to haunt him. He was also afraid Jackie would come upstairs and see her, when she couldn't, or Natalie would wake and haunt his son. But the ghost wouldn't stay with him for long. She struggled around the room, struggled in the atmosphere of the living and grunted in protest while he refused to look at her. As soon as he let the covers down she began her insistent wail, with a note of irritation in it.

"All right, I'm coming," he said nervously, and as soon as he slid his legs out towards the floor she flew onto the window ledge. Though he couldn't see her outline very well he felt sure that she'd had the other children with her, and had come to fetch him so that he could admire them. His collection was diverse, after all, and consisted of little boys and girls ranging in ages five through thirteen, with Natalie being the oldest.

When he moved away from the bed she jumped from the window and ran off at once through the fields, giggling. Toby went downstairs, out the backdoor and ran behind, not thinking at all of the darkness, but full of pleasure because she had left the children alone and unprotected in order to fetch him. Natalie reached the barn ahead of him, and when he switched on his flashlight he saw that she had gone into one of the metal stalls he had put for the horses and to cover the soil beneath it. On her knees, she was tearing away at the dirt with which he had lined it with pebbles and bits of asphalt. He shone the light at her and looked carefully at the torn-up floor, but there was nothing. "The children aren't there, Natalie," he said with a small sigh of relief, tears of thankfulness pricking the back of his head because she seemed to have thought of him, thought of what he did when the moon fell strong across the farm and his family was fast asleep. But, at the same time, to have him know he wanted to be there when the children were awake, and had braved the dry rot and the people who suspected him of kidnapping.

When he squatted in front of the stall and talked to her she took her fingernails away from the dirt and came out, touching his face and answering him in the high-pitched and varied tones of declamation which, for a ghost, was her ultimate marks of attention. "No, Natalie," he said, smiling. "I'm sorry. But you're not under there either."

After a while she went back again to the stall, and when she had torn up a little more dirt and asphalt with her nails, she gave up, then patted it down like a sandcastle and sat beside it. Toby got up, meaning to go to the supply chest along the far wall, where he had hidden a tornado lantern and matches for the occasion, but, as soon as he moved, the girl ran out of the stall, protesting.

"Silly girl," he said, shaking his head. "I'm not going to stay with you all night. And I shouldn't have left this door open. Look at the headache you've given me." It seemed the girl had no intentions of haunting him, and for this he was relieved. There came a point, however, where she pushed him and interrupted, and he said, "Yes, yes… I know. I know I'm not your father. But I was the one who bludgeoned you to death, and from this point on that makes me your daddy. Clear?" But she refused to believe him. She followed him to the supply chest, crying and pleading while he filled and lit the lantern, and she didn't settle again until he had pulled an old spread from a wall hook and curled up on it, where she could see him. After a while he turned the wick of the lantern low, so that the middle of the stall and the girl and her overeager face were lit, and the rest of the dingy barn was in shadowy half-light.

Time passed, and Toby began to shiver a little and to feel slightly sick with the quick excitement of not knowing what to expect. And only when there was a new kid, always at the barn. It was when he had put his head down, though, and closed his eyes that the girl grunted and he looked up quickly and saw that, still sitting inside the stall, she was trying to disappear with effort. Toby sat up and turned up the lantern, anxious to see, to watch, to miss nothing of what was happening. She wailed heavily again, but when Toby put out his hand and grabbed her by the throat, he said, "You can't leave here, Natalie. You're an entity now, thanks to me, and doomed to stay here until somebody frees your spirit." She answered him with the soft shrieks which she'd often used when she was busy wandering the cornhusks, or with the other children. After a few more moments he released his grip on her and she walked out of the stall and sat on the supply chest, and in the faint light of the lantern her eyes were glassy with concentration. Then she began to hover, floating in circles to find a suspicious looking spot and trying hard, with her wisplike body, to locate the graves of the other children. They had to be buried in here somewhere, she felt. For a moment she tried to get a purchase against a slab of wood, boarding off a small niche in the far corner. As Toby turned he saw that the bottom half of her body was lifted high up in the air, her head lowered and gazing inside the niche, and that there was something in the dirt, silvery and shining, showing from just underneath it. Then the ghost grounded herself again, and began to reach for the silvery seeming object.

Toby pulled the lamp closer, and his stomach heaved with revulsion against what he saw and what she was doing. Something had gone wrong. "Sorry, you won't find them in there, Natalie," he blurted out, "try and try as you may." But he had to say that. Glowing from the dust and cobwebs that touched the floor of the dark hole was an ankle bracelet, and with it she could see a small skeletal foot. She pulled on the foot as hard as she could and was eventually able to uncover part of a girl's corpse, but she did not recognize it, for it was not hers. The head looked as if the eyes had been gouged out of it, and what pieces of decaying flesh remained, was soft and pink, quite without hair and structure, crawling with maggots and all other sorts of small insects.

Toby closed his eyes, shuddering, and then he opened them and tried to explain. "All right, I'm sick. I'm a deranged man, what more do you want from me? Even after I gave up farming I wanted another child, someone I could spend my time with. And even after I learned Jackie could no longer conceive. Brad's big now, and he only wants to hang out with his friends. He's grown cold and distant." He stopped for a moment and shed a tear before starting again. "After the first one I wanted another. It became habitual. And my wife would never have allowed it. So I had to abduct them and keep them here until they became a nuisance, and when they became a nuisance I slaughtered them. Still, I was so fond of them, even you. I didn't want to let go, so I figured why should I only collect boys and girls in life when I can also collect them in death?"

When Natalie turned around and touched the corpse it turned into a big pile of dust. "So that's it, that's it," he said to himself aloud. "You're representing the children. As the oldest of the victims you're out for revenge on their behalf as well as your own." Leaning closer, he watched as the ghost's gentle airy hand turned another corpse's skull, cleaning and dusting it off. Now the soft gray hairs that had been invisible to her before began to stand up with a life of its own, like a fuzz of down all over a big, infirm head. It was then that Toby first heard the child's voice since its death—small and angry and whining—as it fought against the push of Natalie's hand with its first, urgent craving to get back to the warmth and comfort of life, in which it was forced to leave behind.

"Please, don't do that," he warned her. She seemed to him to be cleaning it off with wantonness, knocking and rolling the upper half so that the skeleton could be released in its entirety. From what she could tell, this one was a boy.

After a few minutes of frenzied cleaning the ghost settled, but she still reached out to give it a single, confirmatory poke. If she heard crying, then she was doing right. "Aren't you going to dig some more?" Toby asked her. "You can't excavate just one child. Might as well finish what you started." Natalie leaned back against the hole and closed her eyes, and the dust and cobweb-filled niche was occupied with the little dead children's protests and the ghost's own ragged grunts to make them materialize further.

Toby, slightly concerned, brought his knees up close to his chin and folded his arms to make a rest for his head and, after some time in the dim light, in the quiet sound of the boys and girls cries and Natalie's ecstatic wailing, he began to doze.

When he awoke an hour later he found that so much had happened in the barn while he was sleeping that he had to put his hand in the hole and stir through the dirt and take a body count. He found now that there were seven bodies, and the seventh was Natalie's, pushed all the way to the back while he counted the missing parts to the others. Looking outside, he noticed that sunup was less than an hour away. He longed above everything now to be in bed and be free of the madness the ghost was attempting to bring upon him, the return of the spirits of the other children. But he felt that the young ones must have a proper burial, at the very least, and to prevent him from being caught by the authorities or haunted. The nearest cemetery, an old abandoned catacomb for early settlers, was ten miles away. Not too far, but still risky if he was to travel along the river with a plump bag of bones. He found a giant potato sack that he'd used when he farmed fulltime, and went out of the barn with the remains fully packed. It surprised him how daylight came so fast and how the sky was gray instead of black, and he hurried because he was afraid that he might not get back into bed before Jackie got up.

He found the cows all lined up patiently at the gate and waiting to be let out so they could graze. The horses, too, were all out of their stalls and waiting gate-side, wondering when he would let them loose. It would be faster if he rode by horse, he thought, and the palomino his neighbor had sold him some years back could make it at least to the well in suitable time. If worse came to worse, he figured, he could always dump the bones there and be rid of the children for good. But there was the case of Natalie, the ghost with mild yet unfriendly temperament, the novelty of being put in a jam by her. Her inconsistency no longer borderlined on mere attention or revenge, for when he put down the bag to see if he had collected all the remains, hers was nowhere to be found.

When he got back to the barn he found her, and she kept turning her head to stare at what he was doing and then moving off a pace or two so that he was forced to chase after her. "You can't run, Natalie," he said angrily, putting down the sack and going over to his supply chest. "And you can't hide. Don't think because you found the others you can end this. Bringing the children back from the dead won't work. You won't drive me mad!"

He removed some dolls and animals from the chest and placed them on the floor for her to play with, just like he had done for the other children when he had seized them. It was evident to him that if he captured her spirit then he would have no problem securing her bones. The ghost accepted a little of the bait, but she was still somewhat curious, and wouldn't go through with it. "Come on. Don't you want to play with me?" he said. "Why else would you come to my window in the middle of the night?" Once more she picked up some of the bait but put it back down. "Come now, Natalie. You're being stubborn, same way you were stubborn when I blanketed out your voice. Because of you I have to get rid of my collection." But she still wouldn't go for it.

Finally, after a few moments, he left the rest of the toys beside the hole on the floor, shut the barn door and ran quickly home through the gray dawn with his hands and feet aching from sleeplessness, and his mind full of the revelations and manifestations of the night.

Toby slept late that morning, the bag of bones hidden in the closet. It was only when he heard the clatter of plates going onto the table for breakfast that he willingly got up, pulled on his clothes without washing and went out, grumpy and aching, nervous and anxious, to the kitchen.

"Well, look what the sun brought in," Jackie said, as she stood by the kitchen sink. "I didn't see you in bed. How late did you stay up?"

"Not too late," Toby answered. "Busy day helping Bill out with feeding and watering. He'll be screaming by the time I get to the husks. I had a lot on my mind. But nothing to get all worried about."

"Hmm... It's not like you, dear. Usually I'm the one who likes to sleep in."

After breakfast, when Toby had walked his son to the school bus, and he had helped his wife by drying the plates, he went up in the closet and recovered the bag. Downstairs, Jackie saw him with a great big potato sack over his shoulder and asked, "Where are you going with that?"

"Uh... um... to Bill, where else?" And by the time she muttered out her next sentence, he was already sliding around the door to the veranda.

He started off by one of his three different, circuitous routes through the fields to the old barn. He walked slowly across the paddock, unlike the night before, because he was a little afraid of what awaited him there. Jackie's words over breakfast had comforted him, but then she had being talking about her sudden infertility, not about ghosts and corpses on their property.

When he opened the door and found Natalie waiting for him in her usual frightening stance behind it, he was filled with such fear that he couldn't imagine why he hadn't gone to the old cemetery or well with the bones sooner. He put down the bag and reached out his hand, touched her misty face and felt the lean lines of her restored proportion. "Well, someone's been busy," he grinned. "I don't think you have enough power though to bring yourself back from the grave. You're dead, and there's nothing you can do about it." She gritted her teeth in anger and put out her own hand, with its fingernails colorless and full of dirt, and across her lips, as she looked at him, spoke silent threats into his face.

He stepped back then and dumped out the bag of bones on the ground for her in the way she would have wanted it. Then, while she looked through the body parts and made her own count, he went to look for the toys from the night before. However, they were all gone except for a Hug-Me-Tender doll, whose face had been crushed from inside. When he picked it up its squeal made Natalie look up sharply from the bones she was checking, but after a moment she seemed confident that he was doing no harm to other children in the barn. It soon fell apart in his hands, and a chill ran down his spine. He handled each limb separately, looking at the arms, the legs, and even the eyes, going on to say, "Where are the other toys? How did you manage to break this, and in this manner?"

Natalie giggled.

Toby turned around and shot her a dirty glance. "Answer me!"

But there was more giggling.

When she had finished with the last bone, Natalie floated back to the center of the barn, stepping delicately to pass him and settle herself among the *others* in the shadows. Toby seemed to marvel at the forms that now took their place around him, and how they knew at once which way to grope with their hands, while Natalie, who was already on her way to materializing fully, would have failed her friends had she not made *him* the prize offering.

Cornered, Toby looked at the ghosts of the children before him. There was little Lea, five years old, with her Walmart dress covered in ash. There was Brenda Sue, eight years old, still covered in soil and wearing her Raggedy Ann-like outfit. Bobby Joe, seven-and-a-half, with his cowlick for a haircut. Johnny, who would have turned six, his throat torn out and dried blood covering his striped Izod polo. And Diana and Michael as well.

Toby began laughing, but it was more like a whimper, a cry for help. "So this was the plan, huh? Natalie brings the children back from the dead. Save the children, what must be done. I guess that makes you more than a ghost. No, wait! Natalie the necromancer!" He laughed some more, and then he wept. "But what if I don't want to believe in ghosts? What then?"

Natalie stepped between the crowd of little boys and girls and took his hand. "Mister Linderscott," she said gloomily, her vocal chords now able to transmit speech, "I think ya shoulda thought of that before you took us from our real mommies and daddies. Now we have to punish you the same way you punished us."

"I don't believe, I don't believe," he said, pulling back from her in an ecstasy of fear.

The first child reached across from where he had been standing and slashed off a big piece of Toby's ear, and then with a simple touch, burned the fine fair hair that grew atop his temple. The children closed in on him, and they laughed and smiled and delighted as they fed on his soul. He closed his eyes and let the soft, mesmeric hands wash over him; and very soon he became just like them.

Plough Monday
by Tom Johnstone

'So what felony bought you passage in here?' asked one.

'Murder, of course, same as you,' replied the other. 'That's why we's both in the condemned cell.'

'And did you do it?' continued the first.

'What's the difference? I'm going to swing for it. I just hope I die clean, that my neck'll snap like a twig, not a slow lingering death as the noose tightens and my tongue blackens and my eyes start from their orbs...'

'Enough! Let's find more congenial conversation... What wassailing song do you love best?'

'Ah! That's easy... 'Tis the song of Saint Monday, sure as my name's Jack Barley:

> 'St. Monday brings more ills about,
>   For when the money's spent,
> The children's clothes go up the spout,
>   Which causes discontent...
>
> 'And when at last he staggers home,
>   He knows not what to say,
> A fool is more a man than he
>   Upon a fuddlin' day!

'Aye! Many's the Monday night we used to go out carousing to that sweet refrain, clinking our wassail cups before Slugwash Hall. Our cups was overflowing before the Lord of the Manor could be rid of us. And he was happy to indulge us, so long as we ceased our *charivari* once he'd crossed our palms with silver. After all, his bounty kept us content in our toil for the remainder of the week, and moreover, if he treated us miserly, he knew we'd plough up his front lawn!

'But things changed when he quit this earthly realm, and the young master took his place, he of the furrowed brow, that prematurely domed and furrowed brow, above a hawkish nose and thin lips that never smiled, fresh from his time in the city reading dusty books of law. He was hell bent on putting a stop to all our weekly holidays, for 'twas true there weren't a good day's work to be done by any man jack of us 'til Tuesday were dead and buried. Aye, Wednesday were the start of the working week as far as we was concerned, and that was the way it were going to stay, even if he were to send the Justice of the Peace to read us the Riot Act!

'"St Monday brings more ills about", the song says, and it's certainly been my undoing, as you shall presently hear tell, my friend in felony. From the day the cold-hearted Sir Richard claimed his inheritance, their door was bolted to our merry band of worshippers at the altar of St. Monday. There were others we could cajole, but his late father's generosity had always provided the richest pickings for us. And 'twere only fair, considering the beggarly pittance he paid us for our labours on Slugwash Estate. Sometimes it were only the meagre crops from our pitiful small-holdings that kept us from starvation.

'Despite young Sir Richard's hard heartedness, we continued our revelries, but his campaign against our association went beyond his own portals. One Sunday, the first Sunday of Lent it was, on leaving church, I spied him in close conversation with the parson, out of ear-shot of myself and my comrades. But I knew his intent. This was to be a crusade. Sure enough, the following Sabbath, the sermon was a veritable temperance speech, denouncing false gods and especially false saints. He asked with a sneer where in the holy canon was Saint Monday? A mutter went up from certain quarters, and when the collection plate went round, not one stout man put his hand in his pocket. If the parson would conspire with His Lordship to deny us alms, which causes discontent, then why should we pay for the upkeep of his rotten church?

'The next day was Monday, and we decided to pay Sir Richard a nocturnal visit. What though his door be barred? We'd already drunk deeply by the time we reached his gate, and Nutmeg, the pallid, skinny mare, went before us, pulling the plough as best she could. I always drove the plough, save one night I shall tell of presently, for in our mummery, I had been cast in the part of Piers Ploughman. Someone thought it would be fine sport to mark the manor lawn with the ploughshare, just a small furrow as a warning of what was to come if he did not leave us be.

'In the sobre light of Tuesday, I repented that I'd permitted the deed, and I expected to be horsewhipped for sure, since everyone in the village had seen me driving the plough of a Monday. But to my surprise, the expected swift punishment did not come straight away. Instead he delivered a common penalty, to all those of the St. Monday persuasion, that caught us all unawares.

'One crisp, dry night, in late October, I was lying awake. A formless dread was keeping me from slumber. As I was wondering what manner of unease this was, an acrid smell stung my nostrils, the rank odour of smoke. I leapt from my bed, and ran outside, to see all the winter crops on fire! I couldn't see a soul, but I knew it was his doing: Sir Richard. I sounded the alarm, but it was too late.

'After that, it weren't just the childrens' clothes that went up the spout, so did their vittels. Some didn't make it through January. Those that did make it were marked, with pinched, sallow faces, in which a spark had died. It had died in us too.

'The Monday after the crop fire, my associates and I went about our revels with a terrible, hungry desperation. As fate would have it, this Monday fell upon October 31st, All Hallow's Eve, a night when 'tis the custom for poor folk to seek restitution from their betters. We knew we could expect no treat from our Lord and Master, and so it seemed our destiny to visit a trick upon his person. The only question was what form this prank should take. Given the bad blood between him and us his humble tenants, it seemed unlikely that this should be given or taken in a spirit of good humour. But few could have imagined how far certain members of our merry fraternity would go to bring him down a notch or two. Indeed as it turned out, I was never to learn what happened that night, not until I was arrested and charged for the deed one year later.

'The rain was pelting down as we tramped through Slugwash Common, that All Hallows Eve, our boots sodden with wet clay. With my belly empty save for ale, I was already prey to strange fancies. I feasted recklessly on mushrooms, careless of their types and properties, washed down with an evil dandelion liquor brewed by one Philip Dogwood, of whom more I shall relate shortly. Some of the fungi were liberty caps, prodigious things with devil's teats and very strange intoxicant properties, so named due to their resemblance in shape to the caps worn by the *sans culottes* over the Main.

'Perhaps some of the spirit of those stout fellows, who'd made the bloat King Louis and his minions the guests of Madame Guillotine, was abroad that night. I can remember saying that I wanted to plough a great gash in His Lordship's great lawn, and then someone else saying that he'd like to plough a great gash through His Lordship's peevish pate, and after that little more, for this was the occasion I told you of before, the one time I allowed the trusty plough to pass into other hands. I think perhaps I may have feasted on slugs after that, thinking them liberty cap mushrooms. Finally I lay down a while with my face to the heavens, and let the deluge soak me to the skin, until my comrades roused me and mocked me for missing the sport they'd just enjoyed, for they'd kicked an uncommon ball from Slugwash Hall all the way to the copse, they said.

'When at last I staggered home, the effects of the intoxication were beginning to wear off. As I passed the common ground where our crops had been destroyed, I noticed that the ground had been newly turned and no longer seemed scorched and desolate. Someone had been a-ploughing, I could see, for there were furrows all thereabouts. The soil was wet, and not just from the driving rain. It seemed to be mixed with white fragments of some kind - broken crockery or maybe animal bones. And whoever'd been busy working the soil that night had even crowned the plot with a scarecrow. Not that it was much to look at mind – a sorry looking creation with a piece of filthy sacking for a head.

'After that night on Slugwash Common, I thought the spirit of St. Monday had been well and truly laid to rest. With all our Winter crops wiped out, Sir Richard would surely set our noses to the grindstone like never before. We could not feed our families on what we could forage from the hedgerows, and it seemed clear how poaching game would be dealt with under Sir Richard's stewardship.

'But far from ruling the Estate with a rod of iron, he seemed to have become what they call an absentee landlord. There was much gossip about where he had got to. Back to London to resume his studies, some said. Truth be told, there were few that missed him, what though it meant a famishing furlough. Poaching had never been easier, which made up for the want of work and the burnt crops. Spring came, and on May First, as the sack-faced scarecrow looked on, we dragged the 'obby 'oss to the scorched earth that was all that was left of our plot, singing:

'Unite and unite! Let us all unite!
For Summer is a-comin' today!
Whither we are goin', we will join together
In the merry mornin' o' May!

'Now I don't know if it was the 'oss, or what it was, but our crops came back with a vengeance that Summer. I all but asked Nutmeg if she knew something I didn't, for surely she must have been dolloping non-stop all over the soil for it to be so fertile. Or maybe it was on account of that scarecrow, which oversaw the land with a kind of baleful vigilance. Never before did I see one that truly did what it was properly put on this Earth for, which is, scare crows! Usually the crows do show their scorn for your common scarecrow by perching insolently on the ragged effigy's crucified shoulders. But this was no common scarecrow, for the birds gave it and the crops a wide berth. So come the Autumn, that patch of earth was awash with prodigious fruits - great, swollen, bright orange pumpkins the size of barrels, purple-crowned turnips the size of cannon balls, crisp ruddy apples and lush red strawberries the size of my fist.

'But something was wrong. And it had to do with that previous All Hallows Eve on Slugwash Common.

'A few days before the next All Hallows', the anniversary of that night, I found Philip Dogwood setting about his lad with a willow switch. I grabbed his arm, and asked him why.

'"I caught him with this!" replied he. "Thinks it's funny, does he, carving a Jack O'Lantern with a face like that?"

'"Leave the boy alone!" said I. "He meant no harm. Besides, this ain't no carving. 'Tis the shape of the fruit, as Nature intended."

'"Nature?" he screamed. "It looks downright unnatural to me. Look at that face!"

'With its hawkish nose and high, domed forehead, I had to admit the countenance did look familiar.

41

'"But Dogwood," I pleaded with him. "Tis nothing but a gourd, a pumpkin, and these are but bumps and blemishes on its skin. Let's take a look at the others, eh?"

'So I took him to the vegetable plot, him dragging his boy by the ear.

'But when he beheld Nature's bounty, far from calming himself, he screamed and began raving, like one who unwitting spies a Mandrake root. And when I took a long look at that strange and bitter crop, I could not help but think 'twere a whole harvest of Mandrakes.

'There lay hundreds of the monstrous, bloated things, all with the same bumps and blemishes, bearing the same uncanny resemblance to the face we'd hoped never to see again, the face of Sir Richard, but scored by something His Lordship had never been known for in life – a twisted grin from ear to ear.

'This latter feature was even more pronounced in the potatoes.

'I and my fellows was always careful when digging them up, delving around the rows so as not to scar the precious tubers. But this time, when we set about a-harvesting the tatties, no matter how careful we were with our spades, it seemed that not one escaped the blades. Indeed, so badly scarred were they, that they were barely fit for the pot. And each one bore the same two slanting slashes – *in the same places...*

'"He's paid us in his own coin!" cried Dogwood like a petulant child. "Stamped his miserable face on every one, like a King's Sovereign!"

'"You're not making sense, man!" I said, utterly befuddled now. "I reckon as you've been dining on liberty caps, my friend."

'"Sir Richard's corrupted the soil, Jack! Oh, 'tis rich, that soil, full of blood and bone, the best, oh the very best, the finest pedigree!"

'Eventually, the Justice of the Peace sent men to dig up His Lordship's final resting place, though they were kind enough to let us harvest the crops first. Bits of him were strewn all over the vegetable patch. Dogwood and the others must have buried him up to his neck in the ground, and then driven the plough over him. The search party managed to piece together the body from the fragments that had been ploughed into the soil, but the head was a different matter.

'I expect you'll have guessed where the Justice's men found Sir Richard's head. Quite how the flesh still clung to the skull uncorrupted was a fact for which they could not account, for eyes in that head still blazed with a frightful, preternatural malice. It had been doing a grand job of affrighting the crows under that piece of sacking, but had remained fresh enough to attract no cloud of tell-tale flies. This they put down to vinegar in the sacking, but I knows different. On clapping eyes on His Lordship's head, they covered it up again as swiftly as they could. For if that ragged countenance put carrion crows to flight while covered up, naked it loosed the bowels of stout grown men.

'The plough must have taken it clean off. Well, maybe not so cleanly as all that, judging by the ragged, slanting cut on the scrawny neck. There was other such slashes higher up, they say, one disfiguring the domed forehead, and another that stretched the mouth into a ear-to-ear grin, skewed and toothless. It seems that they'd had a few goes with the plough before the share had hit low enough to take the head off.

'Now don't get me wrong. It ain't as if I think Sir Richard's cruelty should have gone unpunished. I'd seen my children crying for food on account of his flinty heart, just the same as everyone else. But this weren't Madame Guillotine. I've heard how that kind lady knocks off the bewigged crowns of your French aristocrats quickly and efficiently as a foxhound nipping sly old Charlie in the neck, most clean and humane-like. Now your English landed gentry are far the most part lucky enough to be spared the justice of the poor, though there have been fears abroad that we wretched of the earth might follow the French example. That is why a man such as I must hang, as a warning to others, for when the poor take courage the rich must take care. But there was nothing noble about Sir Richard's end. 'Twas messy, drunken slaughter. And even after his head had finally and irrevocably been parted from his body, there was no peace for it. This was plain to see for anyone who looked upon it, when they found its jagged stump jammed onto the sharpened middle pole of the scarecrow that kept watch on Slugwash Common. For on the unnaturally fresh head with its unnaturally blazing eyes there bloomed ghastly purple bruises. Something had caved in the skull, which was quite knocked out of shape. By Nutmeg's hooves, or by boots kicking it through the woods by the disciples of St. Monday (who boasted of enjoying sport with an uncommon football)? I'll let you be the judge, sir! But God is my judge, and I'll say no more on this subject, except one final thing: if I had been Philip Dogwood that night, and on so crudely and hideously beheading His Lordship had beheld eyes still blazing in that head, would I not have exhorted my comrades to join me in a game of football, in an attempt to kick and stamp the damned lustre out of those hateful eyes?

'But forgive me if I sometimes wake you with my screams at night, sir. Only some long nights I am visited in slumber by the image of a hacked and battered potato bogie, all stamped with His Lordship's dead features, the domed and furrowed brow, the stumpy remnants of a hawkish nose and a slanting slash of a grin. Though I am guiltless, I still must bear the Mark of Cain within my head.

'And when they came for me, I knew not what to say. After all, I was known for miles around as the keeper of the plough, so when they showed me the share all caked in blood, I had no choice but to present my hands for the irons. It all made no sense at all to me. Until I thought back to what Dogwood had said to me that dank October day in the vegetable patch.

'"You see, Jack, you passed the mantle onto me down on Slugwash Common. I was Piers Ploughman that night!"'

'So why didn't you let them know?' interjected the listener. 'You're going to hang for another man's crime!'

'We all hated Sir Richard,' said Jack Barley. 'So whoever did it, we're all jointly and severally culpable. As for Dogwood, staying alive is more of a punishment than going to Tyburn. And I know for a fact that he'd rather see his children starve than suffer them to eat from that vegetable patch.'

Mask Murderer
by Karen L. Newman

The rustle of shopping bags and the steady hum of voices twisted together to form the screeching chalk on the blackboard of eighties music that blared throughout the mall. Justin Moore disliked the mall and its din. But he disliked not eating more. He sat on a hard stool behind the narrow counter of a Halloween kiosk. It was the only job he could find after he cashed his last unemployment check.

Justin looked up from his magazine in time to see a teenage boy grab a Scream mask and dash down the mall.

"Come back here, you little shit," Justin yelled, knocking over his stool and a rack of masks as he chased the thief. Soon he heard a crash behind him.

"What the fuck is it now?" Justin turned around, his hands on his knees. People surrounded the kiosk like vultures, picking the plastic flesh from its metal bones. He screamed for security as he lumbered back. They scattered, clutching their prey.

Justin mopped his brow with his shirttail. He guessed about a fourth of the masks and costumes were gone. His boss, Mr. Fraley, would have a fit.

A young man in a navy blue uniform approached. "Sir, are you alright?"

Justine barked, "Does it look like I'm alright?" He told the officer what happened.

"Well, sir, I'm afraid there's nothing I can do here. You'll have to come to the main office and file a report."

"And who's going to watch my stuff?"

The security guard looked around nervously and stuttered, "Well, sir, you know, we're short-staffed here, and, uh, don't you have someone you can call?"

An artery popped up on Justin's temple. "You dumb ass, I wouldn't have lost all this shit chasing that fucker if I could've just called some goddamn body."

The young man stepped back. He'd seen this crazed look before when he worked security at *a* local bank. He didn't want to hang around for a hidden knife or gun to appear. "Take it easy, sir. File the paperwork anytime you want. They'll be in the office. Just ask the manager." He turned on his heel and trotted down the concourse.

Justin kicked some masks. Giggles broke his concentration.

"What're you looking at?" he asked the small group of people gathered around the kiosk. "Buy something or leave."

The onlookers scattered like roaches at the flip of a light switch.

Justin wondered what to do as he straightened up the kiosk. He didn't have enough money to pay for the stolen items. And he had to pay. It was in the contract that he signed with Mr. Fraley.

Justin noticed a third of the remaining masks and packages were damaged. He couldn't sell those. He tossed them behind the counter.

He returned to his stool and put his head in his hands. He didn't deserve this. He did everything expected of him. He married his high school sweetheart and joined the local union after receiving his electrician's certificate at the community college. He got on at the motherboard manufacturing plant and worked his way up to foreman. It wasn't his fault that an overseas company bought out the business and the new management laid him off along with hundreds of others. After that, his wife, Amy, left him for his former friend, Jim McClure, who took over as foreman.

Justin pounded his fists on the counter. The jingling of the cash register emulated the sound of his wedding ring clinking around the toilet bowl before he flushed it. He curled his lips. With this job ending the day after tomorrow, he could take the money in the register and leave town. He could make a fresh start.

But before he left, Justin wanted to make Amy and Jim pay and make some money doing it. And he had a plan.

Knowing Mr. Fraley wouldn't return to collect the money until after Halloween, Justin left several hours early. Business was always slow near the mall's closing. Instead of putting the masks and costumes in storage, he carried them to his SUV.

Afterwards, Justin went inside the mall and entered an electronics store. He showed the pimple-faced clerk his electrician's card. The teenager took it and checked it against a list beside the cash register.

"Here, sir," he said, handing Justin his card. "How may I help you?"

Justin looked him in the eyes and replied, "I need some programmable nanoprobes for a job I'm working on."

What kind of job could he be working on? the teenager thought. *I've seen him here at the mall for the past few weeks at the Halloween kiosk. Hell, what does it matter? I have to meet a sales quota.* "Come back here." The clerk led him to a backroom where the nanoprobes were hidden from the public. Justin picked out an assortment. In silence the clerk placed them in a reinforced sack.

They returned to the storeroom where Justin also purchased a programmable remote and an assortment of stainless steel wires with some of the cash from the kiosk. He tucked the plastic bags inside his denim jacket and walked outside.

The cool night air blew wisps of Justin's gray hair over his bald spot. He pulled out his ball cap and pushed the bill down toward his leathery face. He got in his SUV and drove home.

Justin parked outside the low income apartment complex where he had to live. It was the last step to living on the street. Amy had taken the house and all of his money in a divorce funded by Jim. Out of the corner of his eye, he noticed the drug dealers in the shadows along the perimeter of the building. They were like wasps. If he ignored them, they'd leave him alone.

Justin walked with long strides to his apartment, the key in his hand. He opened the door and put the bags on a couch littered with empty pizza boxes. He went into the bedroom and overturned a banker's box full of CDs.

He made several trips to the SUV, filling the box and dumping the contents on the living room floor. He locked the apartment door and worked all night.

Justin arrived at the mall an hour early. He restocked the kiosk with the altered masks that he rewrapped in their original packaging as best he could. To ensure they sold, he marked them half off.
He sat on his stool and waited.

He had sold a third of them when Jim McClure sauntered to the counter and smirked, "Hey, old buddy, how ya doin'? It was great hearing from you last night."

Justin looked up from his magazine and put on a fake smile. "I appreciate your coming here and helping me out."

"Hey, I'm glad you remembered us. These costumes look great. I can't believe they're half off on Halloween."

"Well, they were damaged in shipping."

Jim picked up a rubber Frankenstein mask. "Looks OK. Feels a little hard around the edges, though."

"Like I said, they were damaged. They should fit fine."

"Yeah, yeah, whatever. I'll take all you got. This should be the best assortment ever for the company party. How much do *I* owe you?"

Justin hesitated. He didn't want to get greedy here at the end and ruin everything. "Tell you what, for old time's sake, let's make it an even five hundred dollars."

Jim's eyes widened as he tapped his manicured fingers on the countertop. "Wow. Are you sure? Don't you want to ring them up first?"

"I could, but then you'd be late getting back to work. Besides, the boss wants them gone."

Jim chuckled. "You don't own this kiosk yourself?"

Justin's face reddened. "No, this is just a temporary gig. We only take cash," Justin said when Jim pulled out a VISA card from his Italian leather wallet.

Jim replaced the card and counted out twenty-five twenty dollar bills. "Yessir, I'm really looking forward to tonight. These parties are always a blast. I assume you're going to load this stuff into my Lexus." Jim wanted to see Justin suffer. Carrying all that heavy stuff to the SUV would be payback for all the extra heavy lifting he endured when Justin was the boss.

Justin rang open the cash register and put the money in the drawer. "Sure. It's the least I can do, but you'll have to watch the kiosk while I'm gone. I've had some trouble with theft lately."

"Really?" Jim's bushy eyebrows rose. "Well, you always did have trouble holding onto things." His lips curled and he winked his left eye.

Justin turned to hide his rage. He had to tolerate Jim's remarks or lose his chance at retaliation.

Justin pulled out a box from behind the counter. He filled it with masks and costumes. He faced Jim and said with a cheerful voice he hoped sounded sincere, "I got the first load ready. If I can have your keys, I'll get started."

"Yeah, sure, man." Jim riffled through his pocket and tossed the keys on the counter.

Justin threaded the key ring through his index finger. He lifted the box and marched out to the parking lot. He opened the sliding door of the Lexus SUV with the remote keyless entry button on the key ring. He wanted to throw it in, but thought better of it. He laid it on one of the bucket seats and returned to the kiosk.

Jim stood by the counter next to three costumes. "Hey, Justin, I was just thinking. How'd you like to come to the party tonight for old time's sake? Amy and I'd be glad to have you. And the guys will want to see you again. Don't worry about a costume. I got yours right here." He indicated the Frankenstein costume.

Justin's mouth flew open. Why the one eighty? Then he noticed the other two costumes - George and Laura Bush. His face drained of color. He and Amy hadn't been divorced a year and she was going to marry Jim. That had to be it.

"Hey, buddy, you OK? You look pale."

Justin leaned on the counter. "I haven't been feeling well lately. I've been under a lot of stress. I don't think I'll be able to come tonight."

"Too bad. I might as well tell you. Amy and I are getting married this Christmas. I wanted to tell you first, so you wouldn't have to hear it from somebody else. Sorry about the ribbing earlier. I thought with all your experience, you'd bounce back from that layoff."

Justin knew why he couldn't get a better job. He had asked one of the local contractors why he hadn't been hired and was told Steve Miller, his former boss, had given him a bad reference. Justin had been shocked at the time, but, when he thought about it, should have expected it. Steve's mean streak was infamous at the plant.

Justin lied, "I've got several job prospects lined up after the first of the year. I'm just doing this to get by until then."

"Well, good to hear it. If you can, please come tonight."

Justin's lips curled. "I just might."

After six more trips to the Lexus, Jim and Justin shook hands.

"Good doing business with you," Jim said.

"Likewise."

When Jim was out of sight, Justin opened the register and stuffed all the money but the coins in his pocket. He left the kiosk without looking back.

After he arrived at his apartment, Justin headed straight for the bedroom. He pulled his suitcase out from under the bed and filled it with clothes and beer. He grabbed the remote from the dresser and flung the keys to the door on the kitchen table. He closed the locked door behind him and walked with confidence to his SUV. He threw the suitcase in the back and tossed the remote on the bucket seat beside him.

Justin drove to a hotel on the outskirts of town and parked at the far end of the lot away from the road. He took out a travel clock he always kept in the front pouch of the suitcase. He set the alarm to 7:30 pm, a half hour before the start of the company party. He tilted his seat back and fell asleep.

Darkness had covered Justin like a blanket when he awoke at the clock's beeping. He rubbed his eyes, dazed and confused until he saw the remote. It was time.

He started the vehicle and turned on the headlights. He drove with care across the parking lot and pulled out onto the main road. As he approached his former neighborhood, small packs of children on their way home from trick-or-treating formed disjointed parades down the sidewalks that lined the streets. Justin wished he was a kid again, when his only concern was how much candy he scored on Halloween.

Justin parked the SUV in an alley half a block away from the house he used to share with Amy. He patted down the seat beside him with his fingertips until he found the remote. Ensuring that the shiny red button wouldn't be pressed by accident, he picked it up by the corner with his thumb and index finger and transferred it facing out to his shirt pocket. He held his wristwatch to his bloodshot eyes. Ten minutes until the first guests would arrive. He needed to get into position.

Justin put the SUV keys in his other shirt pocket and unlocked the door. He inched it open as he peered around the corner. He listened for children and barking dogs and heard only the rustle of crisp leaves under his boots as he stepped out. He held the handle while he closed the door to minimize noise.

A cool October breeze tickled Justin's whiskers as he walked down the grassy alley. After several feet, he saw the floodlights perched beneath the roof of his former home. He crossed into the dark yard next door and tiptoed between the trees and shrubs until he found a tall bush in which to hide at the edge of the bright lights. He peered through the narrow spaces between the braches at his former coworkers walking down the sidewalk toward Amy's front porch. Their laughter peeled Justin's nerves raw.

Justin moved his right hand to wipe a bead of sweat from his brow. He jumped at the crackle of the branches near his beer belly. He stood still, his heavy breaths forming a white shroud over his face as he waited to see if someone would investigate the noise. The steady stream of people turned into a trickle, but no one ventured near Justin. After not seeing anyone for several minutes, he dashed across the narrow strip of grass between the houses and rolled under the shrubs planted beneath his former home's picture window. He bit his tongue at the sharp pain of the needles scraping his cheeks. He crawled through the damp dirt on his hands and knees to the edge of the porch.

Justin held his wrist to his eyes and saw that the watch read 8:30 pm. *Enough time's past,* he thought. *Time to make my move.*

Justin scrambled up the steps to the porch and rang the doorbell. His chest heaving, he took the remote out of his pocket and held it behind his back. He listened as the sound of heavy footsteps became louder. The door swung open to reveal Jim, his mouth agape.

Justin smiled. "Hi, Jim. I decided to take you up on your offer earlier today."

Jim stood speechless. He never expected Justin to show up, especially looking like a beggar. Maybe it was his costume. Still, he had to get rid of him quick. The last thing he needed was Justin bellyaching to everyone about how his best friend stole his job and wife, even if it was true. Jim returned the smile. "Hey, buddy, how are you? I don't have a costume for you. I guess we ran out. It's been good seeing you." Jim stepped back, grabbed the door, and pushed.

Justin stuck his boot between the door and the doorframe. He wrapped his fingers in Jim's shirt and shoved him to the floor. Justin held the remote in the air and pressed the red button with his thumb.

Shrieks reverberated throughout the house. Jim got to his knees before Justin hit him on the head with the vase he snatched from the shortened sideboard in the foyer. Justin kicked him in the ribs for good measure on his way to the living room where he watched the macabre play he produced.

Justin smiled as his former coworkers stumbled over the furniture and each other like movie zombies in fast forward. Blood oozed out from around their faces from the nanoprobes that burrowed into their flesh. These same little machines also closed the masks' eye, mouth, and nose holes for an air-tight seal. The factory workers and their spouses clawed at their masks as they fell to the floor and writhed like worms on fishhooks. In several minutes they were still.

Justin took his thumb off the red button and the masks slid to the floor, leaving bright red trails behind them. Groaning from the foyer broke the silence. Justin scanned the room for Jim's mask. When he couldn't find it, he remembered seeing it on the sideboard. He returned to the entrance hall where Jim was leaning against the wall. Justin put the remote on the sideboard and grabbed the mask with both hands. He kneed Jim in the stomach. Jim tumbled backwards. Justin shoved the George Bush mask on Jim's face. Justin turned around, snatched the remote, and pressed the red button. He stepped back and watched Jim die like the others.

Justin checked his watch. It was only ten minutes until nine. He didn't want to dawdle. Someone might have called 911 before becoming unconscious. Careful not to touch the blood, Justin reached into Jim's pants pocket and took out his wallet. He put the paper money his own pocket, but left the credit and debit cards he knew could be traced. He entered the living room and took the same type of cash from the other men.

Justin went into the kitchen, expecting to see Amy wielding a carving knife behind the door. Instead, he saw her prone on the linoleum floor like the others. He let out his breath, incredulous that his plan had succeeded. He dashed upstairs to the master bedroom where he found the women's purses nestled among the coats on the bed. He dumped out the contents and took only the cash. He knew he was leaving his fingerprints, but he didn't have time to be careful. He wanted to leave town as soon as possible. He figured he'd be the prime suspect anyway.

Justin ran down the stairs and out the front door. He was halfway down the porch steps before he realized he left the door open. He returned inside and turned off the floodlights. He closed the door behind him. He couldn't see the steps. He shuffled forward until his foot touched air. He sat down and scooted down the concrete stairs while he held his pockets shut. He couldn't afford to lose the money. When he reached the sidewalk, he lurched forward and stood up.

Justin retraced his steps back to his SUV. He entered the vehicle and locked the doors as soon as he sat down. He started the engine with a trembling hand. He drove down the alley and turned onto the first residential street he saw.

Images of his dead former coworkers flashed like surreal billboards in Justin's head as he traveled through several neighborhoods. The enormity of what he'd done hit him as he pulled out onto the main road that led out of town. He had become a god that night, a deity in charge of not only other people's destinies, but his own. He could recreate that night's adrenalin rush, muted cries and flailing limbs, and the coppery smell of the bright red blood as it dripped onto the carpet to form slow-growing maroon pools whenever he pleased.

Justin rolled down the window and took a deep breath. He was as free as the breeze that caressed his left cheek. He could finally experience what his life would have been like if he hadn't gotten married so young and started work.

Up ahead the headlights illuminated the county sign. As he crossed the line, Justin removed his hands from the wheel and flipped his former boyhood home off with gusto. He yelled, "You have been baptized by the mask murderer. Bow before me, motherfuckers," as he stepped on the gas.

Beneath the Orange Moon
by Christopher Allan Death

The old man sat in his rocking chair, humming into the breeze. He wore a blanket over his legs to combat the elements. He didn't want to catch a cold. Not at his age. And especially not so close to Halloween. He had things to do and people to see before the big night.

Once upon a time, he would have carved a pumpkin, lit a candle, and watched it melt away beneath the waxing harvest moon while children scuttled up and down the street, but not anymore. He'd lived far too long and endured far too many hardships to take pleasure in such menial indulgences.

Pleasure was something reserved for the young. It was something that faded and died with time, like a flower uprooted by the fall. Except this year there would be no pleasure. There would be no happy Halloween parties or children skipping through the streets. This year there would be blood. Blood flowing down the sidewalks, bubbling from the gutters; blood raining from the sky.

So much blood that Lucifer himself would shed tears of sadness.

The old man felt a chill course through his bones. The thought of all that carnage made his old heart flutter. He could hear the cries of terror echo in his mind – a sweet symphony composed through misery and death. And for the first time in nearly fifteen years, he smiled.

"God damn it, Jimmy. Will you turn that goddamned music down?"

Ethan McCormick covered his ears, as if the screaming guitars would make his brain explode.

"I think my ears are bleeding."

Jimmy laughed, adjusted the car stereo. He just had a new sound system installed, so he couldn't help but test its capabilities.

"Sorry. I forgot you don't like AC-DC."

"It's not that," Ethan stammered. "I just want to keep my hearing intact for a couple years."

"Says the guy who wears earplugs at rock concerts," Jimmy laughed.

"Hey, don't get me started. You know I have very sensitive ears."

"Yeah yeah yeah," Jimmy returned. "Cry me a river. Just don't pull that pussy-ass shit this weekend, ok? I got a couple hot girls to come to the corn maze with us, and I don't want you fucking it up."

Ethan rolled his eyes. "Don't worry. I'll leave that up to you. You do the fucking – I'll stay in the car."

"The hell you will," Jimmy snapped. "You're my wingman. I can't go out there without you! Think of all that fine imported boo-tay!"

The last word was illustrated by an imaginative hand movement, and Ethan couldn't help but smile. Sure, Jimmy could be a real asshole sometimes, but he was Ethan's only friend. Everybody else at Flagstaff High treated him like dirt.

"So you with me, bro?"

Ethan released a long sigh. "Yeah. I'm with you."

He hated corn mazes and loud music and anything vaguely related to October 31st, but he couldn't let his buddy down. Jimmy had taken a risk by befriending him, since he was the new kid in town, and it was the least Ethan could do to express his gratitude. Besides, they were graduating next year, so they needed to make the most of their time together.

"Right on," Jimmy smiled, jamming the gas pedal against the floor. "Right fucking on. Now let's get to the diner and have some lunch. I'm fuckin starving."

"You read my mind," Ethan grinned, but despite the wind whipping through his hair and the weekend within his grasp, he still felt an uneasy sensation in his gut. Whether it was hunger pangs beginning to set in, or something far more sinister, he didn't know.

Only one thing was certain – October 31st was going to be a wild, wild night.

Pushing through the glass double doors, Jimmy strode into the corner diner. It wasn't much – just a renovated pub that went under in the 1980s – but it felt like home. He'd been coming to the diner ever since he was in grade school, and not much had changed. It still sported the same mahogany bar and chrome stools, as if remembering a time when happy hour meant twenty-five cent beers instead of endless sodas.

He repressed a sigh and folded himself into one of the adjacent booths. He was going to miss the diner when he went to college. It was one of those sentimental places that he heard old-timers talk about. Up until today, he thought they were just blowing shit out their asses, crying about lost opportunities. Now he knew there was more to it. There were some things that he would never forget – some people he would never speak to again, and although he knew that was inevitable, it still filled him with a deep inner sadness.

"Hey buddy. Why the long face?"

Ethan sat down in the booth opposite him and glanced over the menu.

"What do you mean?" Jimmy said quickly, his mind snapping back to the present. He couldn't let Ethan know he was sad. Jimmy was supposed to be the happy-go-lucky high school junior without a care in the world. That was his linage and he wasn't about to let it slip away.

"You just looked thoughtful, that's all."

"Oh," he muttered. "I must have been thinking about those two girls I told you about. Did you know they're foreign exchange students from Europe?"

"Yeah. You told me on the drive over," Ethan said, although he was clearly more interested in the menu than Jimmy was. Or maybe they were just looking at different menus. The main course on Jimmy's menu consisted of a toned European booty, and a pair of legs for dessert.

Grrrr.

Jimmy was hungry already.

"Could I have your lunch combo, with French fries and a coke?" Ethan said, tearing him away from his youthful fantasies.

"And for you, honey?"

The waitress was a girl named Rebecca. She had long red hair and a pretty face, but no curves. Her father was the town reverend, to boot. That alone was enough to dissuade almost any guy from going after her. Then again, Ethan wasn't like most guys, and he obviously had a crush on her. Jimmy could tell by the way Ethan refused to make eye contact.

"You like her, don't you?" Jimmy asked, once she'd retreated into the kitchen with their orders.

Ethan's face went pale. "What are you talking about?"

"The waitress. Rebecca. You like her."

"No I don't. What makes you say that?"

Jimmy leaned forward. "Look partner. Between you and me, it doesn't take two people to pitch a tent. It's lucky this table has a long tablecloth or your ass would have been grass."

Ethan shifted uncomfortably. "Ok, fine. So maybe I like her. What's the big deal? I mean, her dad's a reverend. Even if he wasn't, she's still way out of my league."

"Sounds to me like you're making excuses."

"Then what do you propose I do about it?"

Jimmy let his jaw hang slack, as if to say, "Duh, what the hell do you think, doofus? Go and talk to her for crying out loud!"

"You think I have a chance?" Ethan whispered.

"You never know until you try," Jimmy said. "Just be cool and whatever you do, for god's sake, don't trip over anything. Girls hate that shit."

Ethan nodded and took a deep breath. "Ok. I got this. Save my seat. I'm going to go say hello."

"Atta boy," Jimmy smiled. "Go put the old moves on that chick. She'll be swooning in no time."

"I hope so," came Ethan's unsteady reply. Then he stood up and waded through the sea of tables.

Rebecca was standing in the corner, refilling water pitchers, hair swept back over her shoulder. Even though she wore the mandatory green skirt and apron, she still looked absolutely stunning. Jimmy would have hit that thing if he wasn't interested elsewhere.

"Order up!" came the voice from the kitchen. "One lunch combo and barbeque burger on the bar."

Jimmy rubbed his hands together greedily. He was starving. He hadn't eaten since late last night because he had to work late at the shop. His employer was a mechanic named Eddy – a grumpy son-of-a-bitch, but a good mechanic nonetheless. Eddy had taught Jimmy everything he knew about car mechanics, but more importantly, he'd given Jimmy the self-confidence to chase his dreams – a trait which was severely lacking in Flagstaff, New Mexico.

Most kids quit school and had a baby by junior year, which Jimmy thought was hilarious. He joked that the only thing to do in Flagstaff was eat, fuck, watch baseball, eat in the dugout, watch more baseball, and fuck in the dugout. An inspiring pastime, indeed. No wonder it was America's game.

"Here you are. One barbeque burger and lunch combo."

"Excellent," Jimmy smiled. He couldn't help but wonder what had become of Ethan. The kid seemed to have disappeared. Maybe he stepped outside for a smoke. No, that wasn't it. Ethan didn't smoke. He was afraid he'd get lung cancer and die at the tender age of thirty-five.

"Where's your friend?" Rebecca asked, setting the plates on the table.

"I'm not sure," Jimmy replied. "I was about to ask you the same question."

"What do you mean?"

Jimmy cleared his throat. "See, my friend has this really big crush on you. He wants to ask you out but he's a little intimidated. Says you're out of his league or something."

"Oh." A blush spread over Rebecca's face. "Well, if you see him again, you can tell him I think he's cute."

Jimmy put his hand over his heart. "Will do, captain."

A moment later, Rebecca was gone, and Ethan poked his head out of the restroom.

"Is she still there?" he whispered, looking more like a ghost than a human being.

"Don't worry Casper, she's extinct," Jimmy laughed. "She said that you were cute, though."

"What? Really?" Ethan took his seat across from Jimmy and glanced toward the kitchen. "She said I was cute?"

"Fucking right. She also said that she would bone you for five bucks, but I told her you're not that type of girl."

Jimmy's laughter was interrupted by a quick punch to the chest.

"I'm being serious, asshole," Ethan growled. "Did she say that or not?"

"Cross my heart and hope to die," Jimmy wheezed. Then, after he had a moment to catch his breath, "God, you're strong."

A day passed, and the old man never left his rocking chair. He just sat there, overlooking the town, watching the sun rise and sink in the October sky. He had work to do in the garden, but there was something about the magical autumn atmosphere that held him in place. It was like a drug pulsing through his veins, dulling his senses, stimulating the pleasure receptors in his brain. He wanted to sit there for all eternity, soaking in the sun's golden rays, but he knew he could not. By tomorrow the town would be awash in a red dawn. A dawn seeped in innocent blood.

With that thought in mind, the man stood from his rocker.

"Hey dude! Rise and shine! Are you ready to go to the corn maze?"

Ethan slowly opened his eyes. He knew that voice. It was Jimmy the douchebag, but how he'd gotten into his room at ten o' clock in the morning, Ethan had no idea.

Ethan lived on the second floor of his parents' house, for fuck's sake! Maybe Jimmy climbed the trellis outside his window, but Ethan didn't really care to find out. He was tired and wanted to go back to sleep.

"Time to wake up, dick whore," Jimmy prodded, smacking Ethan upside the head with a tennis racket. "Today is the day that we become men."

"Good for you," Ethan murmured. "Now let me sleep."

"Sorry buddy. No can do."

Jimmy overturned the mattress with a single lithe movement, and Ethan found himself on the floor, wading in a sea of pizza boxes and febreeze bottles. Any other day he would have leapt to his feet and gotten his revenge on Jimmy, but today he felt like shit. Something about the harsh October sun made his stomach turn.

"Come on, buddy. I have a surprise for you."

Ethan rolled over. "Unless it's a new pillow, I'm not interested."

"Maybe you should look out the window before you decide."

Ethan was quiet for a moment. Then he peeled his eyes open and fixed an angry glare at his unwelcome friend.

"Fine. If I look outside, will you stop bothering me?"

A broad smile spread over Jimmy's features. "Yes. Just one look. Then I'll leave you alone. I promise."

"This better be worth it," Ethan mumbled. He half walked, half stumbled over to the window and looked outside, shielding his eyes from the bright golden rays. He jumped back ten seconds later, twice as fast, as if the sunlight had singed his flesh.

"Holy fucking god, man, what is Rebecca doing out there?" he seethed. "I'm not even dressed. I think she saw me in my boxers, dude! That is not cool!"

Jimmy couldn't contain himself. He burst out laughing, even louder than before. Not just because of the expression on Ethan's face, but because he'd never heard him swear before – at least, not seriously. Ethan was about the most wholesome guy in Flagstaff. He never drank, did drugs, fooled around with girls, or egged houses, which were all popular pastimes in their shitsplat town. He was a model citizen.

"If she saw me, I'm going to fucking kill you!" Ethan growled.

Jimmy rolled his eyes. "Oh come on, Tarzan. You look sexy in those things, but I suggest that you put on a shirt anyway. It could get cold tonight at the corn maze."

Ethan sat down for a moment to ponder the situation, then he stood up, slipped into a green Billabong shirt and elbowed Jimmy in the rips ruefully. "That's for messing up my bed, asshole," he said, and marched outside.

Rebecca was in the driveway waiting for him. She leaned against Jimmy's Firebird with an amused expression on her face, legs crossed. Except this time she wasn't wearing the ugly green uniform, complete with grease stains and frayed hems. No. Today she wore a black Metallica t-shirt and jeans – the kind that hugged her hips and accentuated her figure.

Ethan felt his mouth go dry. He had no idea that she was so gorgeous. He'd only seen her once or twice at school because he wasn't really part of the "in crowd." She had her friends and he had his. Or rather, he had Jimmy. Jimmy accounted for three quarters of his friends. The other quarter belonged to his comic book collection.

"Hey," Rebecca said.

"Hey," Ethan replied.

"I like your shirt."

"Thanks," Ethan smiled. He wasn't even aware that he was wearing one. Whenever he came within ten yards of a girl, his mind went blank.

"So ... ready for the corn maze tonight?" Rebecca asked. "I hear it's going to be the best one ever."

"Really?"

Ethan found that hard to believe. Every year the corn maze was exactly the same. The farmer who tended it – an old man called Mr. Reese – was the most unimaginative bastard on the planet. Mr. Reese lived on a hill outside town that overlooked his cornfield, and every year he ploughed a maze into his withered crop to celebrate the season. He was a crazy old coot – crazy to the core. He almost never ventured into town, and when he did, it was only to pick up groceries at the corner market. Then he would disappear again, hiding away in his little hilltop cottage until his next grocery excursion.

"Um, I hate to interrupt you two lovebirds, but we have things to see and people to do," Jimmy said, breaking the uncomfortable silence.

"Don't you mean 'people to see and things to do?'" Ethan asked. He was glad someone changed the subject. A blush had starting forming on Rebecca's face, and he could feel his knees begin to wobble.

So much for a good first impression.

"Just get in the fucking car," Jimmy growled.

The time had finally come. The vegetables were finally ready for harvest.

Slipping a pair of thick leather boots onto his feet, the old man hobbled out to his garden. He could feel the sun's warm kiss upon his face, and a slight October chill in the air. This was the moment he'd been preparing for since last summer. He'd carefully chosen each and every seed that he planted so they would bring forth the richest, most bountiful harvest ever. And now, thanks to hours of preparation, his garden was filled with giant, glistening vegetables.

He went to the pumpkins first, running his knotted hands over their sheen orange skins. He needed to choose the biggest, most beautiful pumpkin, because that was the most important. The squash and gourds were important as well, but not nearly as vital as the pumpkin.

Running his fingers down the spiny green stems, he finally found the one he was looking for. It was perfect – large, round, and orange, without the slightest defect. Its skin was so smooth that it almost felt like human flesh.

Perfect.

With a quick twist, the pumpkin came free of its spiny umbilical cord and fell into his arms. It was heavy, but nothing he couldn't handle. He was a fifth generation farmer, for god's sake. He could handle more than the average American.

Plodding through the soft earth, he felt a grin spread across his lips. In less than twelve hours, the town of Flagstaff, New Mexico would be aflame with terror. And all because of one wrinkled old bastard.

Setting the pumpkin on the porch, he went inside to fetch his tools. He emerged a moment later with a pencil in one hand, and a steak knife in the other. Its serrated edge winked at him dully beneath the October sun.

He sat down, cradled the pumpkin between his legs, and plunged the knife into its succulent orange flesh. It would be the Jack o' Lantern to end all Jack o' Lanterns.

Piloting the Firebird down the narrow street, Jimmy couldn't help but smile. He had his best friend Ethan in the passenger seat, and three beautiful girls in the back. He couldn't imagine a better evening.

Up ahead, a brilliant full moon rose above Mr. Reese's corn maze, bathing the stalks in a surreal orange hue. Most of the town had turned out to enjoy the festive event, and already he could smell the delicious aroma of popcorn and apple cider in the air.

For Flagstaff, Halloween was more than a holiday. It was a social event, where everyone ventured out of their homes to mix and mingle and have a good time. Even the good reverend was known to frequent the party, but tonight was the biggest turnout ever. People from the neighboring towns were seen dancing, laughing, and eating outside the maze. A few out-of-staters had shown up, too, their license plates illuminated by the waxing moon.

Jimmy stepped out of the firebird and wrapped his arms around the two European girls. They had dark hair and brown eyes – just his type. And what's more, they were European. Fucking *European*. Wasn't it every guy's dream to do it with two European girls? He didn't know, but he had to imagine it was.

Ethan edged out of the car behind Jimmy, wide-eyed, like a deer caught in the headlights. Ever since Ethan had met Rebecca, he'd been quieter than shit. Jimmy almost felt sorry for the guy, but then he remembered he had two *European* chicks on his arm.

Cha-ching.

"So, what should we do first?" Rebecca asked, looking almost as uncomfortable as Ethan.

"Let's go by the snack booth," Jimmy suggested. "That way we can get some hot cider before we head into the maze."

"Good idea," Ethan said. They were the first words he'd spoken since they arrived. "It's going to get cold in that maze. Especially if we get lost."

"I know I won't get cold," Jimmy smiled. He gave Ethan the old I'm-going-to-get-lucky-tonight-and-hopefully-so-will-you wink and started off toward the snack booth.

Ethan and Rebecca fell in behind and shuffled silently side-by-side. Their eyes never met. Instead, they watched their shoes kick dust into the darkness.

"So how's school?" Rebecca asked, shattering the nail of silence that had sealed Ethan's coffin shut.

"Oh, not too bad," Ethan murmured. "It's school. Nothing out of the ordinary."

"Huh."

He walked a few more feet and realized he was supposed to return the question.

"How's school with you?"

Rebecca shrugged. "Not bad. I got an A in science."

"Congratulations."

"Thank you."

"What do you think their names are?"

"Excuse me?"

A smile spread over Rebecca's lips. "Those two foreign girls. What do you think their names are?"

"I don't know. Tweedle and dum?" Ethan guessed. He hadn't meant to be funny, but Rebecca laughed anyway. She had a pretty laugh. It wasn't too high and it wasn't too nasal. Most high school girls annoyed him when they laughed, but not Rebecca.

"Can I ask you a question?"

"Sure," Ethan replied.

"How did you end up in such a shitty little town? I mean, do you like it here? I know it isn't exactly the excitement capital of the world."

Ethan thought for a moment. He didn't know how to tell her that he hated the city, and that little Flagstaff was a breath of fresh air. He didn't know how to tell her that big schools intimidated him, or that he used to throw up every morning before class. So he settled for a little grunt instead.

"Was that a yes?"

Ethan took a deep breath to keep from fainting. "Honestly, I don't know what it was."

High above the cornfield, above the giggling teenagers and the alcohol-induced revelry, the old man had finally completed his task.

Stepping away from the porch, he surveyed his handiwork. The light of fifty candles glimmered in the darkness, slipping out through the crooked smiles and hollow eye sockets that decorated the vegetables.

"Excellent," he breathed, feeling a swell of pride in his chest. His minion of Jack o' Lanterns smiled and frowned back at him, each one terrifying and beautiful in its own way. He'd carven each one individually, so no two were alike.

Tilting his head back so he could see the giant October moon, he spread his arms wide and opened his mouth. The words that followed were a mixture of ancient incantations, Latin phrases, and mythical spells. He'd spent months memorizing them, so he could perform effortlessly when the time came.

Closing his eyes, the old man remained perfectly still. The wind picked up around his outstretched arms, and seemed to form little tornados of darkness around his fingertips. The power of his words caused the heavens to split open, and an ominous crimson fog drifted through the clouds.

"The time has come," he whispered. "Tonight the good Lord will punish all those who live in wickedness."

"Hurry up you guys! We don't have all night!"

Jimmy ran forward, dragging his two femme fatales close behind. He was excited, and for good reason. Once he got a good distance into the maze, he was going to bust a move and get busy with his two foreign hotties. The thought sent a chill up his spine.

Once again, Ethan and Rebecca brought up the rear. They shuffled along, sipping their apple cider and exchanging genial small talk when the silence became too much to bear. They didn't have much in common, but that wasn't surprising. Ethan was a city boy, born and raised in Chicago, whereas Rebecca was a Flagstaff native – the daughter of a Baptist reverend.

Ethan took one last drought of his cider and tossed it into the cornfield. He loved Jimmy, but the guy could act like an ass sometimes. At the moment, Jimmy seemed to have disappeared into thin air.

Ethan tried to quell the rising nausea in his gut. This was the last thing he wanted – to be alone with Rebecca. Forget *Nightmare on Elm Street*. This was ten times worse than anything Freddy Kreuger could cook up.

"Are you feeling ok?" Rebecca asked. "You look kinda peaked."

"Yeah, I'm ok," Ethan replied. "I'm just cold, that's all."

"Oh. Maybe I can warm you up."

"Maybe. Er … what?"

Ethan turned to look at her, but nothing could have prepared him for what he saw. Rebecca had unbuttoned her flannel shirt, and was in the process of removing the black Metallica one beneath. He felt his heart skip a beat. Her skin was so pale in the darkness, it almost looked like paper. Lush, warm paper that slid closer until it was mere inches from him.

"What is it?" she purred.

"N ... nothing," Ethan stammered. "You're ... you're ..."

"The reverend's daughter? Yes. But I have a naughty side. Would you like to see it?"

"I think I already have," Ethan swallowed. He could smell her perfume now – it was sweet and seductive – like a Victoria's Secret billboard ad. Except the underwear he was currently studying wasn't made of ink and paper. They were made of fabric, and they were slowly coming loose.

"M ... m ... maybe we should wait," Ethan stuttered.

Rebecca's eyes flashed. "Why wait when you can have me now?" she smiled, and tackled him into the cornstalks.

High above, lightning flashed and thunder rippled, crawling through the iron clouds. The old man held his arms high, undeterred by the tornados of darkness that enveloped his fingertips. He could feel an electric pulse simmer through his bones, but there was no pain involved – only euphoria.

"Yes. Yes!" he muttered. "The time has come! Rise my children! Rise!"

A moment later a thunderous clap split the heavens, and a red mist swarmed over his cottage. He could see vague shapes in the fog – monstrous faces and gnashing teeth – but he was not afraid. He knew the minions of hell couldn't harm him. He'd released them from their spiritual bonds, and tonight, for the first time in a thousand years, they were free to roam the earth.

A wicked light danced in the old man's eyes. He watched as the red vapor swirled above his home, and began darting into the maniacal Jack o' Lanterns. The candles sputtered and dimmed as the demonic entities entered their newfound bodies, and in a blinding flash of lightning, something wondrous happened. The Jack o' Lanterns began sprouting arms and legs – hideous appendages that looked more animal than human.

"Ha-ha-ha-ha!" the old man laughed, his lips curled back in a ravenous snarl. His children had come to life. They had entered the realm of the living, and were ready to shed human blood.

The day of reckoning had come for Flagstaff, New Mexico.

Wading through the giant cornstalks, Jimmy felt his heart skip a beat. He couldn't imagine a better night. All his dreams were coming true. He was busy following a trail of lingerie through the darkness, and soon he would be waist deep in two European hotties, rolling aimlessly in the corn.

Apple cider and sex. There wasn't a better combination.

"Hey girls, wait up!" he called, feeling sweat roll down his brow. "I'm getting tired back here!"

He paused, listening for an answer, but there was none.

Maybe this is some sort of weird European ritual, he thought. *Maybe they want their men to sweat so they'll have a salty personal lubricant.*

Jimmy smiled. If Ethan was around, he would tell Jimmy to shut the hell up.

Suddenly, he heard a rustle in the bushes to his right. He stopped running, and put his hand to his ear. There it was again – this time closer. Maybe the two vixens decided to stop running, overcome by his roguish charm.

"I can hear you, sweetheart," he purred in his most romantic voice.

The sound stopped abruptly, as if frozen in place.

"Come on out, honey. Let the Jimster show you a good time."

He waited, but heard nothing in response. The night was quiet – quieter than a tomb, and just as murky. A vile black fog began seeping through the cornstalks, running through the yellowed leaves like molasses. It was cold, and sent a diabolical chill down his spine.

Something strange was going on ... but he didn't know what until he pushed through the veil of cornstalks. There – on the muddy ground – lay the two femme fatales. Their skin was bleach white, and a trail of bubbling red liquid sprouted from their naked breasts, forming a kind of macabre lingerie.

Jimmy wanted to scream, but when he saw the beast perched over their prone bodies, his throat seized up. It was horrific – like nothing he'd seen before. Monstrous gray arms sprouted from its oblong head, bony and fastened with long, wicked claws that danced in the breeze.

"Jesus save me," he sputtered. That was the last thing he managed to say, because the monstrous being lunged, Jack o' Lantern fangs barred.

Across the field, Ethan had problems of his own. Rebecca had knocked the wind out of him when she tackled him, and now she sat happily on his chest, running her hands up and down his abdomen.

"M … maybe we should think about this," he wheezed, struggling to regain his breath.

"I don't think there's anything to talk about," Rebecca smiled, the words dripping from her lips like poison. "I know you like me, and I like you too, so let's just leave it at that."

"Um … that doesn't mean we should get … ah … physical," he sputtered. "We should get to know each other first. Go out for coffee, see a movie, that sort of thing."

Rebecca's eyes narrowed. "Ethan?"

"Yes?"

"Do me a favor and shut up."

"Ok."

Ethan felt his brain begin to lock up. That happened whenever he was forced into an uncomfortable situation. And this was one fucking uncomfortable situation. On a scale of one to ten, it was a twenty, and there was nothing he could do about it. He had a one hundred thirty pound girl sitting on him, for god's sake, and a lung without air.

"I like feeling your muscles," Rebecca whispered, leaning in close.

Ethan wanted to laugh, but he could feel her breath on his cheek. Her ruby lips dangled precariously above his, shimmering in the moonlight, threatening to drop at any moment. And they did. But not before Ethan felt a warm liquid spread over his belly.

At first he thought Rebecca had spilled her apple cider, but when he looked into her eyes, he knew that wasn't the case. Her pupils had become small and foggy, and her lips trembled, as if in great pain.

"Ethan," she squeaked, and then fell forward, her face landing in the mud. A crimson stain spread over her back and slithered onto his chest, like a living waterfall. Above him, a giant creature stood, flexing its pitchfork-like fingers and barring its crooked jaws.

"Oh my god," Ethan stammered, struggling to free himself from Rebecca's cold embrace. The being was some sort of a demon, borne from the depth of Hades, with a pumpkin head and legs that twisted to the ground like hairy vines. He tried to scream, but like his recently deceased friend, Jimmy, he found himself unable.

The creature reached out and plucked Rebecca off the ground, turning her limp body over in its razor-sharp talons. A stream of blood gushed from the ragged hole in her back and created a pool in the muddy earth.

The sick bastard was admiring his handiwork.

Ethan leapt to his feet while the creature was preoccupied, and stumbled into the corn. He wasn't going to sit there like a drunken idiot and let the creature disembowel him like it had disemboweled Rebecca. He was going to take his chances and try to escape.

Truth be told, he thought he *had* escaped. He thought he'd dodged a bullet, and that he was home free. But that was before a heavy object hit him in the chest and left him gasping for breath, covered in mud and blood and fear. That was before a furrowed old man materialized through the cornstalks and put a heavy leather boot on his chest.

"Holy shit," Ethan sobbed, not just because he was afraid, but because this was the second time he'd had the wind knocked out of him. And he didn't like it one bit.

"What do you want from me?" he cried, as threads of lightning split the sky above.

"I don't want anything," the old man grumbled. "You have proven your righteousness."

"What ... what are you talking about?" Ethan cried. Raindrops began falling from the sky, coating his face and washing the blood from his chest.

"This town was saturated in sin," the man snarled. "Tonight that evil was purged from its midst."

"Then it was you!" Ethan gasped. "You're the one who beckoned those ... those demons!"

"No," the man said firmly. "It was your pathetic little town. They called this judgment upon themselves through a life of debauchery and sin. I merely aided its coming."

"How?" Ethan spat. "How did you get those ... things to appear?"

A jumble of questions rattled through his mind, but they were the only words he could will himself to say.

"Tonight is Halloween," the old man said with a steely glare. "The night when the wall between our realm and the spiritual realm is the weakest. All I did was fashion bodies for the demonic entities to possess."

"But why now? Why not twenty years ago?"

"Because the town was not evil enough until tonight. You see, demons require sin to survive. They cannot take physical form unless there is enough wickedness around them. They thrive on human depravity."

Ethan swallowed slowly, trying to digest what he'd been told. The old man took his foot off Ethan's chest, allowing him to breathe freely, and began to recede into the cornfield. But before the old man could disappear entirely, Ethan struggled to his feet.

"If demons thrive on sin, why wasn't I killed?" he called.

The man paused, and turned slightly. The rain had slicked the white hair over his forehead, and had begun to run off his wrinkled brow. He looked more like a corpse than a man.

"Because you are innocent," he said.

Those were the last words Ethan heard the old man say, because the next day he disappeared, leaving the local police department to clean up the carnage.

Half the town died that night, on October 31st, 2007, including the reverend and his daughter. It was an event that Flagstaff, New Mexico, did not soon forget. Yet, as the years passed, and memories began to fade, old sins began to show their hideous faces, and Ethan McCormick wondered if one day, he would be called upon to follow in the old man's footsteps, and rid the town of its inherent evil.

The Devil's Grotto
by Sam Leng

"Delivery!"

Six-Six-Six Purgatory End; the house's name, not the number. A young man, mid-twenties, struggled with a stack of pizza boxes. His face, poking around the corner of the pile, was acne-scarred; his forehead chafed as a result of the worn rim on his bicycle helmet. He had just yelled his all-too-familiar call into the intercom of a gloomy detached building that he had never actually known existed. He shivered abruptly. It was October 31st and freezing.

"Ahh… De-Livery!" An aged man in a hooded black housecoat threw open the front door. "Welcome to my humble abode, young chap. I see you have brought my supper! How very kind of you. What's your name, my son?"

"Blake," the delivery man replied through clenched teeth, and attempted a weak smile. He had no time for pretentious old fools. This was his last call of the day. A Dracula costume beckoned, along with a night of alcohol-fuelled parties. Apple bobbing? Perhaps. Seduction efforts? Most definitely. White make-up would hide his unflattering complexion, and in a disguise he was bound to feel more confident with women.

"Could you bring the food inside for me, do you think, Mr. Blake?" The man in the doorway asked. "I'm sadly frail, and would most likely drop it all. I wouldn't want you to have endured the long journey for nothing."

This was true; it *had* been a long journey. Purgatory End was difficult to locate. If it hadn't been for the detailed directions the customer had left it was doubtful Blake would ever have found the address at all. The mansion-sized home was surrounded by acres of land on the outskirts of the city. It was only marginally within Preen

Pizza's free-delivery area. A few yards further and he could have declined the job, or earned a small bonus.

With tentative steps, Blake followed the man inside and placed the pizza boxes - all seven of them - onto a round wooden table in the hall.

"Why thank you, son," the homeowner said, digging his thin, gloved hands into the pockets of his coat. "Now tell me, on this fine Halloween night, would you like a trick or a treat?"

Blake had never really understood the point of this question. What right-minded individual would ever request a trick? His Halloween fun as a child had been marred because of this philosophy. If ever a subject of his trick-or-treat endeavours had eagerly responded 'Trick', Blake would hastily retreat back home, fearing the person may be psychotic. Because of this paranoia, in the present moment, Blake hurriedly replied "Treat".

"How wonderful!" The customer declared, flexing his shoulder muscles. "I have got the perfect treat for a young man like you!"

The front door of Six-Six-Six Purgatory End slammed shut. Blake quickly regretted his answer.

The man with red-tinted skin offered punch and pizza. Blake refused. He had always worried the sadistic few who opted for a trick were crazed and unstable. Now his suspicions had reversed. The customer had introduced himself as Granville. Granville the Devil. Granville the Beast. *Granville the Stark Raving Mad.* Somehow, despite his wizened appearance, he had managed to overpower Blake, tie him to a wheeled chair and subject him to a tirade of horrifying notions. Those notions went something like this...

"For years, every Halloween, I have been collecting Living Souls. With so much Heavenly magic on Earth - miracles, if you will - I'm afraid I've become rather jealous and envious. Sitting on my throne in the fires of Hell is a fine way to kill time, but after a few billion morose spirits have passed through into the Underworld, I must confess that my interest does start to diminish and turn to boredom. As a pizza delivery man, I'm sure you can relate to this. What are you? Twenty five? Some men are married, earning thousands, and thinking about starting a family by that age. But you? Well! For a short while you may feel a certain pride in taking care of the pizzas, but at the end of the day it's not the most interesting of careers, is it? Don't you wish *you* were one of those lucky guys who have everything?"

Blake had grunted at this point. In agreement, but secretly. He didn't want to make his own hang-ups too obvious.

"In any case, this is about me. Whatever *you* feel about *your* sad life is irrelevant. *I* want more. I don't want to settle simply for terrorising the dead. I want to try out my talents on the living. But that's difficult alone. I'm not really all that terrifying, as you may have noticed. Sure, I have horns, rose-coloured flesh and black, frequently exploding welts, but compared to most Earthlings this, I think, is rather attractive. Besides, I can only leave Hell on All Hallows Eve, when everyone is dressed up like me, or one of my ghoulish advocates, anyway. So, you see, I hit a snag."

The snag, evidently, was where Blake came in.

"I intend to forge an army of '*undead*' beasts to wreak havoc on Earth, purely for my own amusement. But I am no natural conjuror. To fashion this army I need resources. One thousand Living Souls. One thousand Halloweens. *One thousand years*! And can you guess what is special about this wonderful night?"

Blake had moaned solemnly to himself, which prompted Granville, yet again, to answer his own question.

"Of course! It is indeed the one thousandth Halloween! For a millennium I have been planning this night. And finally my wait is over. You, young Blake, are the final Living Soul for my army. Does that not feel more satisfactory than living your life as a dull delivery man?"

On this note, Granville bit into a slice of Hawaiian pizza with extra pineapple.

"Rubbery," he grimaced, "and fairly cold. I'm afraid you can't charge me for this."

Spurred on by his own quip, he launched into an adapted first stanza of Clement Clarke Moore's Christmas poem. Evidently he thought of himself as an alternative Santa Claus.

'Twas the eve of All Hallows, when all through the house
Wicked creatures were stirring, preparing to pounce.
The army had formed a fine phalanx with care

Knowing the final soul soon would be there!

"You may come to my Grotto now, where all the magic happens," the Devil informed Blake. "We will settle the arrangement once you have met your comrades!"

"No!" Blake voiced his emotions for the first time. "Please. I own up to not being entirely happy as a pizza delivery man. It's true, my ambition and motivation are not what they should be, but I'm supposed to be at a party now with beautiful women dressed as ravishing vampires and alluring witches. Do you really want me to miss out on such an event after admitting your own boredom?"

Granville smirked. "Good try, young man. I admire your efforts. However, I have plenty of dark beauties for you to witness. Come now. I'll show you."

Without untying Blake, the Devil took hold of the back of the chair and veered the delivery man onto a waiting stair lift at the end of the hall.

"These contraptions are for old folks," Granville acknowledged as the pair began their ascent, "and I'm sure I'm the oldest of folks who will ever use one. I don't really need it, but it's convenient. Traipsing up and down the stairs in these strange Earthling buildings is tiresome. Hell is all on one level, you see. Much easier."

The stair lift jarred as it reached the top of the flight of steps. Granville wheeled Blake into a large darkened room to the left of the landing. It was deathly quiet until the Devil flicked the light switch, then instantly the room became equally deathly loud. Nine hundred and ninety nine winged demons, standing in a perfect phalanx formation, screeched and cawed. They wore a millennium's worth of different fashions, and appeared almost human, except for their huge scaly wings and their skin, which was as pale as freshly fallen snow. So pale, in fact, that in parts it was semi-transparent.

"*These are Living Souls*?" Blake gasped over the ear-splitting squeals, while the Devil admired his 'army'.

"Indeed they are! My children. I'm mightily proud of them all!"

"Well they don't look very *living* to me. You can see through most of them!"

Granville scratched his head and turned to face Blake. "You thought my army was actually going to be *living*? I mean, you expected *living human beings*?" The Devil guffawed. "And how would that work, then? A living spirit? Unheard of, even by me!"

Blake felt confused and couldn't concentrate with such a high-pitched racket ringing in his head. "So why call them *Living Souls* if they're not *living*?"

"Hmm..." Granville was puzzled by Blake's interest. He didn't seem at all afraid. Over the years the Devil had come to anticipate many different responses to his Grotto; terror, blind panic, sudden vomiting, pant wetting, loss of voice, fainting, incessant screaming...These reactions seemed entirely normal. Up until now, however, he had never encountered curiosity. It was rather pleasing to him.

"They are called Living Souls, my son, because I acquired the soul while its corresponding body was still alive. Dead Souls, which come to me in their millions in the Underworld, are no good for creating armies. They are already weak and despondent. Wouldn't you be, if you had just been turned away from Heaven and condemned to the pits of Hell, doomed to toil in its fiery work yard for all eternity? Oh, I believe you would."

Blake believed it too, and wondered if he had ever done anything so terrible in his life that might have earned him such a horrifying fate.

"But *you* needn't worry about that! *You* are a Living Soul."

The delivery boy frowned. "Again," he said, "how can they be *Living Souls* if they're not... *living souls*? Am *I* still living? Or do I look like *them* now?"

So many questions! The Devil was delighted.

"I *acquire* the souls when the bodies are living, and when the bodies die I can *use* them. Because the souls were already rightfully mine, they do not have to endure the trauma of making the arduous journey into the bowels of Hell. Therefore, as far as spirits go, they're fairly upbeat and feisty.

And, no, at this moment in time you do not look like them. Not one bit. You look exactly like a pizza delivery boy, with a bad facial complexion and scruffy clothes, tied to a wheeled chair. You do not even look frightened. Why is that?"

Blake considered this. He had been afraid when the Devil had bound him to the chair, and almost scared rigid in the hall listening to his - His? - Hellish ramblings. But now he felt...fine, really. Absolutely fine.

"I suppose my life was more dull than I had ever imagined," he answered eventually. "This is exciting, I guess. A bit of an adventure. And now I know you're not going to kill me..."

"Excuse me?" Granville was stunned. "Who said anything about not killing you?"

"You did. You said you acquire the souls when the bodies are living, and wait for the bodies to die before using the souls in your army."

"Ah!" The Devil grinned. "I see we have our wires crossed! It's perfectly true that I can't use the souls before their bodies die, but I certainly don't wait for that to happen. Why, I'd be here forever! The process must be aided, of course. Hurried on its way, so to speak."

"So you've murdered nine hundred and ninety nine people in as many years and got away with it?"

Granville grimaced. "'Murdered' is such a strong word. Besides, how can death be murder if it is consensual? And even if my actions *are* considered murder in this peculiar living world, who do you think is going to prosecute me? I'm the Devil, for Hell's sake! I dispose of the bodies; I have no fingerprints or DNA; I'm untraceable! And even if I wasn't untraceable, no one would dare testify against me anyway. There are no laws for the Devil on Earth."

Blake sagged in his chair. He was feeling weary. If this all-too-polite beast was going to kill him he wished he just get on with it. What was he waiting for? "And what do you mean by consensual?" he asked ,over the continued squawking of the demon army, which his ears had now adapted to.

Granville grinned and strode towards a desk opposite Blake's chair. On the tabletop a pile of papers were weighted down with a red ceramic tile. He returned with two stapled sheets and a ballpoint pen.

"I'm going to need you to sign a contract," the Devil told his final soul bearer, "to grant me immediate after-death access to your soul."

Blake snorted. "I'm not signing my afterlife away for anyone. You're welcome to kill me, but you're certainly not having my soul."

"Robert Johnson did it," the Devil pointed out, bewildered by this refusal. "Why shouldn't you?"

The screeching of the soul army had become even more acute, though it was impossible to say how this could be so. Blake's throat stung as he battled to be heard over the noise.

"Robert Johnson got something worthy back in return! He was the greatest blues musician who ever lived. What am I going to get? Murdered! That's what!"

"Why must we always resort to this foul word," the Devil moaned. "I much prefer '*helped along*'. And you *will* get something in return. Infamy, a night of total freedom, a guarantee that you will never have to step foot into the boiling basement of Hell. At sunrise tomorrow you will simply dissolve into the atmosphere and rest in peace. This is a very rare opportunity. Is it not rewarding enough?"

Blake bit his lip until it started to bleed. Had the other captives all agreed without qualm to this arrangement? Was he just being over precious about his monotonous life? After all, he had already recognised that his existence was fairly tedious, and his soul had never been much use to him anyway. He didn't even know what a soul was supposed to do. Squeal relentlessly, it seemed. Blake's soul had not yet had a chance to squeal. Should he simply sign the contract and release it to the Devil?

"Fine," Blake conceded. "Untie me and I'll sign."

Granville's face, quite literally, lit up. A small flame flickered with excitement in the centre of his forehead. He extinguished it with his left index finger before unfastening the rope that bound Blake to his chair.

"I'm thrilled you have decided to join us!" The Devil exclaimed. "It's been so long. One thousand years! Can you imagine such a length of time? And now you know my intentions, I would have been forced to killed you anyway. Such a waste of a young life, it would have been."

Blake shrugged himself free of the twisted fibres. "This young life is no waste!" He declared with bravado. It was not the most heroic announcement, but it would do.

Swiftly, the delivery man tumbled out of his seat in a bodged forward roll. His head ached from both its collision with the floorboards and the throbbing commotion which now emanated from the army. He stood shakily to his feet, took a moment to steady himself, then turned to face the baffled Devil.

"May I ask why you decided to throw yourself on the floor, my son?"

Blake's body formed a defensive stance. "May *I* ask why you forced me to bring you seven pizzas, before capturing me and torturing my brain with your *ghastly* ideas?"

Granville shrugged. "I needed a way to get you inside. If I'd simply ordered one pizza there would have been no reason for you to enter my premises. Anyway, I happen to like pizza. I can endure the rubbery texture, and heat them up in the microwave. I will eat them all later, when the show begins. Your delivery efforts have not gone unwarranted."

"There won't be a show!" Blake screamed. "At least not tonight!" He dived blindly for the door, cracking his shoulder against its frame, aware of the Devil's gaze boring into him, probably thinking he was foolish and immature. He rose again. Stumbled. He was almost over the Grotto's threshold and back out onto the landing... Then he collapsed. A non-existent weight pinned him to the splintery floor. One of the Living Souls had intercepted his escape. The room was suddenly silent.

"This is Amelia," Granville said. "She's rather beautiful, don't you think?"

Blake glanced up at his assailant. The Devil was correct. The girl was striking; twenty-ish, he suspected, with dark tresses of hair and deep, sorrowful eyes. She wore a ghostly costume consisting of a tailored bodice and an ankle-length skirt. Her skin was even paler than the other spirits, and she seemed to disappear entirely in parts. Her scaled wings were magnificent, and fanned a cool draught down onto Blake's flesh each time they twitched.

"My name is Amelia," the demon spoke.

Blake was shocked. Her voice was as sweet as honey. He had never imagined these Living Souls had the ability to speak at all, let alone so delightfully soft. Slowly, she continued.

"I was the very first army member to be enlisted in the Grotto. For a whole millennium I have waited for tonight. The Devil is not a terrible beast. He is damned to a life of monotony. Day in and day out he listens to the souls of cruel Earthlings wail incessantly about the perils of Hell, and the hardships of their afterlives. One day a year, at Halloween, he is able to escape this way of life. But what is the use of escaping if he has nothing to do? We are his project. I cannot begrudge him of that, but now, like him, I desperately crave a taste of freedom. The boredom I feel has become simply unbearable. You are my only hope of achieving freedom this year. Otherwise I have another three hundred and sixty five days to wait. I would be devastated should this be the case. I am not sure I could bear it."

Blake felt ashamed. His only aim for the night had been to meet a hauntingly beautiful woman. He had done exactly that, but had selfishly attempted to deny her true freedom. He nodded sadly to the demon, who allowed him to rise to his feet.

"I'll sign," he told the Devil, truthfully this time. "On one condition."

"Go ahead," instructed Granville.

"I wish to be partnered with Amelia in the phalanx. I wish to fly with her, to terrorise with her... And then I wish to diminish with her."

"A demonic love story!" The Devil was thrilled. "This will be a fine vision to witness while I'm chewing on my rubbery pizzas! Indeed you *can* be partnered with Amelia." He handed Blake the contract and the pen. "Just sign away your soul and your wish is my command!"

Blake took a deep breath and scrawled his signature without bothering to read the contract in full. The details, he was sure, had already been explained. He would die, rise as a Living Soul, then die again and be at peace. He handed the contract back to Granville.

"But wait!" He had remembered an important issue. "How will you kill me? I wouldn't want it to be painful."

The Devil smiled, placed a tender fingertip on Blake's larynx, and began to chant:

> "'Twas the eve of All Hallows, when all through the house
> Wicked creatures were stirring, preparing to pounce.
> The army had formed a fine phalanx with care
> Knowing the final soul soon would be there!
>
> The contract was signed in spite of all dread.
> The clauses were clear in the final soul's head.
> And Amelia was happy she had met a bright chap
> Who, for her love, would endure a neck snap!"

A dazzling light illuminated the room. Blake arched his back and slumped to the floorboards as a sharp pain clutched at his body. Screaming was impossible, and pointless anyway. This was a consensual death. Not murder. The Devil had just helped him along.

"From bricks and mortar great cities are built!" Granville roared triumphantly. "Now rise, my child. Rise and join Amelia!"

Blake's lifeless body did not stir. Instead a modified replica, deathly white and winged, rose from the static corpse. The two Living Souls - Blake and Amelia - linked arms and joined the front line of the demon phalanx. The time had come to please Granville.

The Devil nibbled on a slice of Quatro Formaggi and gazed out of the window at his army of children. The one thousand strong swarm of Living Souls blacked out the moon with their great beating wings, then swooped down into the cities of their imitators to shock and petrify. It had been a hugely successful Halloween for Granville, and he now looked forward to spending another millennium plotting a similar amusement. Indeed, the whole challenge had been vastly entertaining. And strangely moving, he realised, as his eye caught Blake and Amelia pirouetting through the sky. Come morning they would evaporate into nothingness, the same as the rest of the ghoulish army, but for now they were soul mates twirling the tango of demons. Their dance floor was Hell on Earth.

Left Behind
by Kris Ashton

Nostalgia takes a powerful hold on all of us from time to time, and in hindsight it was sentiment that drove me to uproot my young family and transplant it in the Central Coast town of Terrigal.

Some of my earliest memories resided in Terrigal: splashing through shorebreakers, hunting crabs in the rockpools, getting burnt crimson in the January sun, visiting the take-away shop in the evening to replenish our energy with hamburgers and milkshakes. Mum and Dad took my brother and me there every summer until Trent reached his teens and grew out of his parents' company. Being five years his junior, I considered this (and his newfound interest in girls) quite mad. But Trent's new attitude coupled with my parents' increasing affluence put an end to our Terrigal trips. Family holidays began to move further afield into other states and finally other countries. I enjoyed these adventures too, but none took root in my mind the way Terrigal did.

I would learn, in time, not to trust childhood memories. I guess if you have enough good times, you forget the lonely hours where parents want to relax and elder brothers don't want to play with their annoying siblings.

The second catalyst for change was a stabbing at Mount Joseph High School. Neither of my children, Jaynie and Ian, would need concern themselves with high school for six and seven years respectively, but the school was only three suburbs away from ours and I began to indulge presentiments of their doom.

When I broached the subject with my wife, Helen, I expected her to resist. We had, after all, only moved into our first house six months before Jaynie's birth.

She did say, "Are you serious?" but it was a genuine rather than rhetorical question.

"I think so," I said. "It wouldn't be that much of an upheaval and it could be good for all of us. You work from home anyway and we could probably find a house with a better workspace for your designs. We" – meaning the agency I worked for – "have an office in Gosford and I'm sure Doug could arrange a transfer for me."

"What about the kids?"

"Well ... they're young. I'm sure they'll grumble a bit at first, but they'll come to love it. What kid wouldn't? And if it means we don't have to worry about them every minute of the day..."

We talked it over some more during the next fortnight. Helen not only came around to the idea, I think she favoured it as much as I did. We brought Jaynie and Ian in on it as well, careful to point out the negatives as well as the positives. Jaynie made some objections to leaving her school friends behind but seemed satisfied so long as she could visit them now and then. Ian, however, showed grave concern.

"Will we still get to see Nana Bragg?" he asked, speaking of Helen's mother.

"All the time," I said. "We'll only be an hour's drive away and you can ring her up whenever you want."

Ian's face relaxed and he nodded. "Okay, then."

With full family agreement, Helen and I spent several weekends scouting properties while my parents minded Jaynie and Ian. On the first Saturday we arrived, I had not been to Terrigal in more than twenty years. The past and the present clashed like cymbals as I took in the traffic lights watching over widened streets, the hulking apartment towers that stared out to sea and the plastic sign board that announced every department store hiding out in the new shopping centre. It reminded me of the first photo I saw of my father as a teenager; the familiar facial and physical referents were there, yet overall the person depicted was a stranger.

I withheld my disquiet and followed Helen's directions to the open house. We needed just five minutes to decide it was wrong for us, so we went to find some lunch before attending a second inspection a few streets away. Joy infused me as I found the old take-away shop, unchanged but for some minor renovations and new neighbours. When I was a kid, a man with a gray goat beard had run the fryers and hotplate. Now a jolly Greek man had taken his place, but the atmosphere remained the same -- the same smells, the same light-green tiled floor, the same clientele with sea-salty skin and bird's nest hair.

Helen and I bought a burger apiece and went to a bench table over the road to eat them. When we were done we still had forty minutes to kill before the second house inspection opened. "I want to go check something out," I said to Helen. "Are you up for a walk?"

She nodded. Hand in hand, we crossed the road again and I took the first right after the take away shop. I had not followed this route in well over a decade, but I thought I remembered it well enough. We followed the street all the way along until it dog-legged around to the right. Second house along from the bend, a simple weatherboard shanty built up on short stilts – that had been the Quinn holiday residence.

I stopped and stared at the new dwelling, the buzz of cicadas drilling into my head.

"What's wrong?" Helen said.

"It's gone. I knew my parents sold it four years ago, but I thought..."

"It was here?"

I nodded. It was not long gone, judging by the newish design of the replacement house, but gone was gone. It was almost as if this home had sprung up out of the ground like a cement-rendered mushroom and upset all the memories kept in trust there. I think I might have gazed at it all afternoon, only Helen squeezed my hand and said, "Well, nothing lasts forever, I suppose. We can make new memories with our own children in our own home. It's still a lovely town."

That cracked the spell and I smiled at her. "You're right," I said.

I took one last look and then we started to walk away.

"Paul."

"Yeah?"

Helen glanced at me. "I didn't say anything."

"Didn't you say my name?"

"I didn't say a word." She grinned. "The sun must be getting to you. Come on, let's go to this other open house."

I shrugged, shook my head, and kept on walking.

We fell in love with the third home we inspected, a comfortable, open-plan house built during the early 1980s. We got in a bidding war with another couple at auction, but they were from up north and did not have the same property value backing them in their old house. We had to go a few thousand above the listed price, but nowhere near what we would have paid.

We moved in eleven weeks after the idea had come to me, mid December. We hired removalists to do most of the heavy lifting, but we still faced a full day of packing in a fierce early summer heat. By the time I opened my third box with a Stanley knife, my shirt had Rorschach blots of sweat back and front. Ian and Jaynie 'helped' for the first hour or so but then boredom started to set in.

"Dad, Jaynie pinched me!"

"I did not you liar!"

"Jaynie," I said, "don't pinch your brother."

"I didn't! And even if I did, he deserved it. He's a little booger-snot."

"Shut your face!"

"You shut your face!"

I attempted to lift a box by its flaps and one of them tore off. It contained, of course, fragile crockery. The children forgot their quarrel long enough to laugh at me.

"Right, that's enough," I snapped. "Go to your rooms or go outside!"

"But I want to help!" Jaynie protested.

"I could do without your brand of help right now. I mean it -- into rooms or outside."

Jaynie took the first option and Ian the second, both sulking as they went. When they were gone, Helen gave me a reproving look. "That was a bit of an over-reaction, wasn't it?"

I rooted through the plates and bowls. None appeared to be broken. I swiped sweat from my face and stood erect. "Yeah, I guess you're right. I'm just hot and uncomfortable and worn out. I'll apologise to them later."

Helen smiled. "How does a glass of lemonade sound?"

"I don't know how to make an effervescent sound, so I'll just say it sounds like a brilliant idea."

Helen kissed my ear (probably the only non-sweaty part of my face) and went to the kitchen. I began to take out handfuls of crockery, stacking them up on the floor so we could remove the sheets of newspaper between each.

"Why?"

Ian sounded sad. I didn't look up. "Why what?"

"What was that, love?" Helen said coming out of the kitchen.

I stood up and looked around the box-filled room. Ian was nowhere to be seen.

"Was he in there with you?"

Helen looked perplexed. "Was who in there with me?"

"Ian. I could have sworn I heard him say something."

Helen arched an eyebrow and handed me a glass of lemonade. "I think you'd better drink this before you pass out. You're probably dehydrated."

I was thirsty ... but I didn't think I was parched enough to hallucinate.

I drank my lemonade and got back to the task at hand.

When I dragged myself out of bed on the Monday I wished I had taken leave time to recuperate from the house move. My back ached, my hands were sore and my brain had yet to recover from the ordeal of pest inspections and building inspections and auctions and contracts in duplicate. Yet as I got in the car, facing only a half-hour drive in moderate traffic, it all seemed worth it. En route out of Terrigal the sea was to my left and the morning sun decorated it with gold foil. Fit-looking residents jogged along the esplanade, others walked their dogs unleashed on the beach. No one seemed stressed or hurried or angry or worried.

Starting my new job was not like starting a new job at all. I knew two or three of my colleagues through work-related phone conversations and it was more like a reunion than an introduction. My modest desk sat side-on to a window that overlooked Gosford's main road. I smiled as I put my briefcase on the desk and clicked it open.

My smile faltered. I quickly took all the documents out and checked through them. Nothing had been stolen – quite the contrary in fact, something had been added. I put the documents back in the briefcase and pushed it to one side, then took the crumpled piece of writing paper and smoothed it out on the desk. Written in the centre of the page in blue biro was:

You left me

The unsteady handwriting was somehow familiar, although I couldn't place it right then. It wasn't Helen's; she had a hand so neat it approached calligraphy. It wasn't Jaynie's either – I knew hers from all the early attempts at printing she had brought home from school. Ian was only just learning to form his letters properly.

I was still puzzling over it when a rotund man approached my desk, his face open and bright. I recognised my new boss from the inter-office website and hurriedly stuffed the note into my briefcase's lid pouch.

In the day's hectic course I forgot all about the note. Only after dinner, while the four of us were zonked out in front of the TV, did I recollect it. I fetched it and brought it back into the lounge room.

"Who left this note in my case last night?" I said, holding it up.

"Not me," Jaynie and Ian said together, their eyes never deviating from the goggle box.

Helen showed more interest. "'You left me.'" She smiled. "One of your old girlfriends?"

I caught her flippancy and jiggled my eyebrows. "Or one of my new ones. No, seriously – I have no idea where this came from, although the handwriting does look familiar. Do you recognise it?"

Helen scrutinised it and shook her head. "It's probably been in your case for months and just turned up now. You know, like a sock that goes missing in the wash cycle."

I grunted. We both knew my briefcase stayed too tidy and orderly for that.

An ad break ended and our show came back on. I put the note on the coffee table and decided to think about it some other time.

I did not think about it at all until two days later. I arrived home from work late, about six-thirty, with a brain that felt sautéed in peanut oil. New names and responsibilities buzzed around in it like blowflies. I wanted nothing more than to sit down to whatever sumptuous thing Helen had sizzling for us and eat rather than think. The last thing I wanted was to walk into the study, turn on the light and find *Freddy* scrawled across the wall in red crayon. I dropped my suitcase from knee height and stormed out to the kitchen. Ian and Jaynie were at the table colouring in.

"Who drew on the wall?" I barked.

My children's pencils froze and they stiffened in their seats. Their eyes grew large.

"I didn't," Jaynie said.

"Not me," Ian said.

"Well now," I said, injecting soft, reasonable menace into my voice, "I know Mummy wouldn't have drawn on the wall and I haven't been home all day. That means one of you is lying."

Ian and Jaynie glanced at each other. I glowered at them, pressing for a confession.

"Paul--"

"I've got this Helen."

"No, you haven't got this," she said, abandoning her pots and walking over to me. "They've been with me since I picked them up from school. They were watching television with me while I was ironing and they've been in here ever since that."

"Well it didn't just appear there by magic, did it?" I said. "You weren't watching them the whole time while they were getting ready for school, were you?"

"No, but I was in there from about ten o'clock onwards. I think I would have seen it then, don't you?"

The name was scrawled across the wall in three-inch high red letters. A myopic pensioner couldn't miss it and Helen had twenty-twenty vision.

I looked back at my kids. "Do you promise me that neither of you did this? If you lie and I find out, there'll be real trouble."

They both nodded vigorously.

Helen looked nervous. "What's going on, Paul?"

"I don't know," I said. "But I think I should call the police."

I did call the police that very night, the act of a sane, rational man who fears for his family. Yet as I dialed the number and made my report to the constable, the primitive, irrational part of my brain had begun to quiver like the wire in a blown light bulb. The name Freddy somehow seemed familiar, yet I couldn't place it.

Two policemen turned up the following morning, just as I was leaving for work. According to Helen, they dusted the doorknobs for fingerprints, examined the message printed across our study wall and took my note away for examination. They also asked lots of questions, pressing Helen to think of anyone who might be aggrieved at our family or have reason to stalk us.

"They seemed disappointed when I told them we didn't have any enemies," she told me that evening. "I don't think they're very confident about finding out who it was."

"Well, if 'Freddy' was still skulking around the place he's probably seen the cops and decided to make himself scarce by now."

Helen shrugged and nodded. "You're probably right. Well, I'm afraid you'll have to cook for everyone tonight. *Junior* has shortened its deadline and I have a thousand words to write by tomorrow morning."

I kissed her. "Have fun," I said as she headed for the study. I wondered whether having bright red letters at her elbow might not distract Helen from the intricacies of bottle versus breast feeding and minimising first-day-at-school trauma.

My own workday had been pretty full-on again, and after making dinner, delivering a dish to the study and keeping the kids amused at the dinner table, I collapsed into the lounge and let the tight spring of my mind unwind. I got to thinking about the name Freddy again, but still the familiarity would not solidify into remembrance. Freddy Krueger, from the *Nightmare on Elm Street* movies? No, that wasn't it. Freddie Mercury? He hadn't even spelled his name the same way. The world supported many Freddys, but none of them could bridge the brook between inkling and inspiration. I fell asleep, still running through lists of men named Fred.

I woke a short time later to my son shrieking. I sprang from the lounge and started to run before I was fully conscious, a kind of sophisticated reflex arc. Hot blood and narcotic adrenaline surged into my brain as a second cry emanated from Ian's bedroom. I almost crashed into Helen as she bolted into the hallway and we continued along at a stilted gallop, like contestants in a cruel three-legged race. Jaynie, who had emerged from her own room, was first on the scene and she stood at Ian's door with a sort of awe-struck revulsion. I squeezed past her and fell to my son, who was on his knees like a Muslim in worship. Fat tears glimmered on his scrunched, purpled face. His left forearm now made a small right-hand turn about halfway down. Helen hugged Ian and began to stroke his head. Rather than mollify him, this coddling only made him bawl louder.

I asked him what had happened but two hitches and a scream summed up his response and a warning glare from Helen put paid to further enquiries. The four of us made our way out to the car and I drove to Gosford Hospital, Ian wailing the whole way like an ambulance siren.

We were fortunate to find casualty almost empty (another tick beside our new lifestyle choice, I thought) and spent only ten minutes in the waiting room before we were admitted. Jaynie, who had been silent up to this point, found her voice again and asked the doctor a breathless stream of questions, only pausing in her inquisition when Ian's arm was reset and he shrieked in agony. The doctor, young enough to be an intern, fielded Jaynie's questions with a kind good grace.

We set off home an hour after we arrived, all sharing a serene post-shock mood. Ian looked upon his slung arm with pride and listed all the people he would have sign his cast in the coming days.

"So how did this happen?" I asked again. We were stopped at a set of traffic lights and I looked at my son's reflection in the rearview mirror. His eyes were downcast.

"Someone pushed me," he mumbled eventually.

"It wasn't me!" Jaynie said.

"No, Jaynie didn't do it," Ian confirmed.

I felt my brow knit up. "So who did do it, then?"

"I don't know."

Helen and I exchanged a look. My wife shifted around in her seat so she could face Ian. "Tell us exactly what happened, Ian."

I could sense his miserable expression. "I can't," he said after a while. "I'll get in trouble."

"I promise you won't get in trouble. Right Daddy?"

"Right."

"Well ... I was jumping on the bed," Ian began.

"Ah," I said. He was a repeat bed-jumping offender and only his amnesty stilled my tongue.

"I hadn't been doing it long," he added, "and then someone pushed me and I fell off."

"Who pushed you?" I said.

Ian thought this over. "I don't know. It was like ... invisible hands."

I remembered a similar feeling as a child, while bouncing on a trampoline. When you're five, your balance and co-ordination are traitors as often as allies. Yet when I tried to put a knowing smile on my face, it wouldn't stick.

That name Freddy rose up in my mind again, unexplained but insistent, like a telemarketer trying to hawk a product without disclosing what it was.

It kept up its coyness as I slid into bed later that night and put my arm around Helen. She snuggled back into me, determined to get some sleep for the busy morning ahead.

We had no idea how busy that morning would be.

"He's mine."

These two words woke me, but only just. My body had taken a full hour to gear down into sleep and it did not want to rev back up again. I half-opened one eye to see dawn's first gray shades softening our dark bedroom.

"What did you say?"

Helen gave no response and I wrote it off as random sleep talking, closing my eye again. Slumber had almost claimed me once more when Helen snuffled and then gave a tight-throated wheeze that ended in a cough. I opened both eyes this time and rolled over to look at her.

"Are--"

The rest of the sentence jammed up in my throat and a cool wave of gooseflesh rippled over my shoulders. A small child huddled over my wife's face, his knees tucked in at one ear, his hands crossed over at the other and his small stomach smothering her face. It could have been any other five-year-old boy, Ian even, except that a thin ethereal glow outlined his body. He seemed to sense my wakefulness and looked up at me from his nefarious work. A tiny blue star flashed in each eye.

I might have sat there stunned and mesmerised indefinitely, except that Helen made a strangled gasp and began to thrash around.

That switched me on like a disc-sander and I sprang to my knees, swinging a huge, looping backhander at the child's face. I half-expected my fist to pass through him, but there was a slap like a cricket bat hitting an apple and the boy fell off the bed screaming.

Helen sat up with a start, holding her nose. "What the hell are you doing?"

I lost sight of the boy. I darted my eyes around the room, cursing my pathetic nocturnal vision.

"We were best friends!" said a muffled voice.

From under the bed.

"Get up, Helen!"

"What? What the hell--"

"I said get up!"

I used both hands to bulldoze my wife out of bed. She stumbled and fell against the wall, rattling the timber blinds. "Paul, you're scaring me! What the--"

"It's Freddy," I said, putting my own back to the wall. I stared at the bottom of the bed, my imagination working in tandem with the darkness to give every shape false movement.

"What are you talking about?"

I swallowed hard. "It's Freddy," I said. "He was my imaginary friend."

"You were just dreaming," Helen said. "There's--"

"He tried to suffocate you."

I heard Helen draw breath to say something but then she stopped, perhaps recalling her airless lungs upon waking.

"Turn on the lamp," I said.

Helen reached over to the nightstand and clicked in the lamp's button. Sick yellow light infected the room. I fell into a slow crouch, now wishing I had a snail's telescopic eyes. On all-fours, I lowered my head until I could see beneath the bed. I made out a pale lemon rectangle of the opposite wall and a strip of cream carpet that turned an ashen gray in the bed's shadow, but nothing else.

No Freddy.

I had begun to believe Helen was right about sleep hallucinations when something filled my left eye's peripheral vision.

I fell back and raised my arm just in time to deflect the downward slash of a carving knife. It cut a deep gash on the outside of my forearm and I cried out, scrabbling backwards and kicking out with both feet at the same time. "Get away! Get away from me!"

Freddy lunged in and one of my bare feet caught him square on the sternum. He fell back squealing, the knife flying out of his grasp.

"Paul!" Helen said, putting her hands on my shoulders. "Paul, what are you doing?"

I turned my eyes up at her. "What do you think I'm doing?"

She gave me a concerned look. "You're yelling and kicking out at nothing."

I got to my feet and put the gaping wound on my forearm in her face. "Does this look like nothing?"

She clapped a hand over her mouth and screamed into it.

"You mean you can't see him?"

She shook her head. I turned my full attention back to Freddy. He had vanished again.

So had the knife.

"Stay here," I said to Helen. I began to creep around the bed's perimeter, taking panther-like steps.

"Oh, God," Helen whispered. "Be careful."

I had reached the foot of the bed when Jaynie appeared in the doorway, a teddy bear tucked beneath one arm. "What's going on?" she said.

My blood turned to red ice. I was only six feet from my daughter but it felt like we were at opposite ends of the Great Dividing Range.

"Get out!" I cried. I lunged for the door and slammed it in Jaynie's bewildered face.

"Daddy!" she shrieked through the plywood.

"You don't--"

The tip of the knife cleaved through my calf muscle and went so deep it clicked against my shin bone. Shock paralysed my senses and I could not even move my eyes. A second or two later the paralysis let go and I turned around to see Freddy wrench the carving knife out of my leg. A dribbly blood jet spurted out onto the carpet. Helen screamed and I fell back, half-fainting with the pain and the shocking contrast of scarlet on cream.

Helen ran around the bed to where I lay and started kicking the air, saying in a furious high-pitched yell, "Leave him alone! Leave him alone GODDAMN YOU!"

She could not know Freddy now stood in the small wedge of floorspace between me and the wall, the carving knife's surgically honed edge resting against the soft skin of my throat.

"You left me behind," he said. He applied more pressure to the carving knife, enough to nick the skin covering my Adam's apple. "We were best friends and then when you went and got other friends you left me behind and never thought about me again."

"Where is he?" Helen cried, kicking wildly at the air. "Paul, where is he?"

I shut my eyes, certain I was about to be murdered on the bedroom floor of my new home.

"I'm sorry," I whimpered. "I'm sorry Freddy."

I felt the knife lift up and I steeled myself for the fatal downward plunge, praying that my imaginary best friend's rage would not extend to the rest of my family.

When after a few seconds I could still hear Helen fuming and ranting and swiping at the air, I opened my eyes and saw only the two of us in the room.

Through a dry throat I cawed, "He's gone."

She stopped in mid-kick and stared at me. "What do you mean he's gone?"

"I said sorry and now he's gone."

Helen's face broke up and she started to cry. She continued to cry as she stripped a sheet off the bed and wrapped it around my wounded leg. On the other side of the bedroom door I could hear Jaynie crying too.

When Helen went out to call an ambulance, Jaynie ran in and threw her arms around my neck. My head began to buzz, my faced numbed up and black nebulas spumed out in front of my eyes. I fought these symptoms and did not surrender until Helen came back into the room.

We did not move out that week or even that month, but we sold up when we could and moved back to Sydney. Sometimes, I think, it's best to let memories be memories.

Hunting
by Aaron A. Polson

On Halloween morning, two young men walked through a gently rolling field spread under a dead, granite sky. The thinner man, Alan Williams, walked deliberately with slow strides, balancing his shotgun at a relaxed angle across one shoulder. Lonnie Jaeger walked thirty yards away, just on the other side of a stand of crooked prairie grass. Lonnie's steps were quicker – he was shorter than Alan – but much broader in the chest, a physical reminder of his years as a linebacker in high school. The lonely country washed away in all directions, only broken and marked by the scribbled lines of naked, leaning trees. Hunting season didn't officially start for another week, but Lonnie's uncle owned the land.

Lonnie stopped and the wind sighed – a long, lonely sound that grew from the grass at their feet and swelled all around. Alan looked at Lonnie, and Lonnie, in turn, glanced across the tall pile of grass at his friend. Lonnie pointed two fingers at his eyes and then poked them forward, indicating a mound of grass about twenty feet in front of him. Alan shivered; the wind was still, but his neck crawled with a little cold tingle that had nothing to do with the weather. He looked to Lonnie again, noting the scratchy net of brown trees along an old creek bed. Something shimmered in the trees – a white flicker like piece of paper blown in the wind.

Two sharp jabs, the calling cracks of Lonnie's shotgun, sounded in his ears, and Alan blinked hard and swung his face toward the sound. Lonnie stumbled through the grass, chasing a haggard covey of quail.

"Damn!" He slid two shells into the gun with sharp clicks. "I almost had those little bastards." He turned and looked at his tall friend. Alan's attention had drifted back to the ragged trees. "What the hell are you doing?" Lonnie asked.

Alan shrugged. He moved his head to the side, halfway facing Lonnie and maintaining a cursory lock on the trees. "I thought I saw something."

"Saw something, hell. I just saw a whole mess of quail fly off into the sunset." Lonnie stomped through the swishing grass to a spot near Alan. "What are you looking at? What did you see?"

Alan shivered again – this time from the wind as it threw another gust across the field. "Something floated in there." He pointed with the end of his shotgun. The breeze brushed the golden grass into flowing subjugation like a sea of admirers bowing to their king.

"Check it out quick. We gotta turn around and get back before I turn into some kind of pumpkin."

"Damn, you're whipped, Lon." Alan laughed. "I'm sure Mel won't care about a little extra quality time with yours truly." Still, he felt a small twist of jealousy in his stomach. Before Melissa, Lonnie would have been the one who wanted to linger on a hunt.

Lonnie's face burned red. "All right, smartass. Let's see what we can find."

Both men, clad in brown save for their orange hunting hats, nearly vanished into a small thicket of cottonwoods and brown, dying pines. The trees clustered around a dry creek bed, following the curving line off through the soft hills of northeast Kansas. Neither spoke as they walked; the only sound became the crinkle of leaves and occasional crackle and snap of a stray twig or stick underfoot.

"No fence. This still must be Uncle Rick's land." Lonnie squeezed between two leaning trunks. Ahead of him, Alan halted just on the other side of the trees. A few dark grey stones lay about almost as if they grew, mushroom-like, from the ground. They were tombstones, showing their age with mottled grey faces and the discolored remnants of moss and vine. Lonnie let out a thin whistle, a slow bleeding sound of surprise. "A cemetery?"

"Just a family plot. Rick know about this?"

"If he does, he never said anything. Let's see the name on the big one." Lonnie took a step past the first row of smaller, anonymous stones. He brushed across the face of the large marker, the family marker. "Looks like Morton…or maybe Morlan. Can't tell."

Grey pressed around the two young men, and Alan looked up, muttering something almost inaudible as he realized they were surrounded by trees, not on the other side of a tree line at all. "Dude, this is a clearing. Only enough space for the little plot." Alan laid his shotgun down next to first row of stones, rubbed the face of one, and squinted to read the battered relief. "These are the kids...Zachariah...John...Jacob...Rebekah. Good old pioneer names, huh?"

"I can't really read the dates on any of them. How do you know they're the kids?" Lonnie asked as his shadow crossed in front of Alan.

"The little stones in the front were always for the children." Alan looked from one end of the row to the other. "Ten...damn. I know it was common to lose kids young, but this had to be rough."

"Spooky shit for Halloween. Look, let's go, okay? I wanna try and bag some birds before I gotta jet." Lonnie spoke as he backed toward the trees.

"Yeah...sure." Alan reached for his gun and noticed a slight flicker on the surface of one small marker. "Lonnie, I though you were going to turn into a..." he began, but stopped when he noticed that Lonnie was halfway through the trees. Something whispered in Alan's head. The sound didn't start with the wind, couldn't have. Gnarly trees built a wall around the clearing and blocked the breeze. Alan heard his name. He shuddered and suddenly realized he wasn't alone.

"Hello, Alan," she planted in Alan's mind. The woman was plain; her hair, eyes, and even clothing seemed to be woven of the colors of the trees, mud, and grass all around. Something in her eyes held sadness deeper than the dead autumn world surrounding them. Alan's body burned slightly, like a light electric shock, and then he was numb.

"Hi." The word dribbled from his open mouth. The woman moved closer to Alan, almost floating rather than walking over the rugged ground. In Alan's brain, he understood that this woman shouldn't be there, but he was paralyzed – transfixed in her steady, dark gaze.

"Alan. My children..." The woman's face shimmered like a flash of sunshine on a small pond. Her thin hand slipped through the air to Alan's chest as she touched him lightly. "We need your help."

Alan closed his mouth, swallowed, and tried to squeeze his eyes shut. His body wouldn't obey; his brain screamed. Even through the layers of clothing, her fingertips stung with a cold snap, a quick burst of ice that spread and seemed to crawl into his chest. The woman's black eyes swelled. "Where is your friend? Did he leave you?"

Two quick pops sounded in the distance. "Lonnie," Alan muttered, and his head snapped to the sound. He felt dizzy, staggered slightly, and caught his motion with the shotgun butt on the ground. When he turned back, the woman was gone, and the clearing silent again with no wind, no more whispers. Alan collected himself, and plunged through the woods back to the open field.

As he tramped out of the shadows, he spotted Lonnie about sixty yards away. Just a dark silhouette crowned in orange from that distance, Lonnie jutted one arm in the air and waved madly. Alan started toward his friend. While he walked, the woman's voice began to bore into his memory like a hungry worm. Alan's knuckles whitened around the stock of his shotgun.

"Where the hell you been?" Lonnie asked with a hint of frustration in his voice.

Alan opened his mouth. He intended to say something about the woman, but she couldn't be real – he must have imagined her despite the memory of her touch and the pull of sadness in her eyes. "Just…taking my time," he quietly.

"Well, I got a couple while you were fartin' around," Lonnie said as he held up two plump male pheasants, their bright feathers shining under a small slice of sunlight that forced through the clouds. "What the hell is wrong with you anyway? It looks like you're asleep." Lonnie stuffed the birds into his hip bag. "I probably better go. You snooze, you lose, buddy."

Alan nodded. The two men trod back through the dead field to Lonnie's truck.

"Look, maybe we can get together again next week, see if we can bag some more birds. If you come home again, you know." Lonnie pulled off his orange cap and smoothed his ragged blond hair.

"Yeah, maybe," Alan said as he looked back across the field and found the small stand of trees that sheltered the graves. "Maybe we can come back again." He didn't want to admit it, but he had a sudden, overwhelming urge to return; to climb through that veil of trees and kneel before those headstones.

"Shit!" Lonnie exclaimed as he looked at the clock in the truck's dash. "I told Mel I'd meet her for lunch at eleven. Let's go, slacker." Lonnie hopped in the cab and slammed his door.

"What the hell's been eatin' you?" Lonnie asked as he steered the truck onto Alan's street.

"Nothing. Look, have a good week. I'll give you a call," Alan said. He spoke into the windshield, not looking at his friend.

"Yeah. Lighten up a bit, okay? Have a helluva Halloween"

Alan nodded, then poured from the cab of Lonnie's truck, pulled his gun case from behind the seat, and waved goodbye as Lonnie hit the gas and growled away. The sun had disappeared again, and the grey sky grew heavy, pressing in around Alan as he shuffled to the front door of his mom's place.

"Mom, I'm home," he announced when he pushed open the front door.

His mom, a short, graying woman with big owl-eyed glasses, stepped out of the den and rounded the corner. "Just in time for lunch, are you hungry?"

"No, not really."

"Much luck today?"

Alan looked down at his gun case. He opened his mouth, intending to try and explain what he saw – those old graves, the woman – but his tongue wouldn't obey. His brain was stewed, lost in a heavy haze. "No, no luck, Mom." He looked into the kitchen at his left. "I'm not really hungry, either." He placed a foot on the first step leading to the upstairs and his bedroom. "I think I'll just catch a nap before I have to drive back to school this afternoon. I figure I'll pick up some candy and wait for some trick-or-treaters tonight."

"Are you okay, Alan?"

He forced his facial muscles into a smile. "Yeah, everything's fine."

The blinds were tightly shut in Alan's room. He would need to leave that afternoon to make it back to his apartment, unpack his clean clothes and prepare for the week's classes. He lounged on the bed with eyes open, feeling like he had been injected with mud, a mud in which the woman's touch still writhed. Time passed, and her voice grew louder. The blinds quivered. She stood in his room like a pale shadow. The odor of brown leaves and cold air swirled around his head, taking him back to the field.

She floated toward him, blue and black now instead of the earth tones she wore in the morning. Alan's heart stirred and began grating against his ribs, but he couldn't force any other part of his body to move. The woman's face inched closer to Alan's, her cold lips brushed his, and they kissed. The chill stole through his body, shaking down through his arms and legs and into his toes. The woman's face was smooth and beautiful, her dark eyes fading into a deep blue. "Help us," she whispered like an icy frost in his ear "the children." The blinds snapped and she was gone.

Alan sat up, trance-like, and pulled on his boots. He looked across the room at the basket of clothes his mother had neatly folded; his eyes glanced over his desk at the picture from senior prom. Alan and Lonnie smiled in tuxedos; Melissa held Lonnie's arm.

Alan snatched the phone from his desk and dialed Melissa's number. He knew it by heart, knew Lonnie's usual routine. Melissa's parents always visited her grandmother in the nursing home on Sundays, which meant Lonnie would be there. His brain throbbed with Lonnie's name.

The phone rang. No answer. Alan let it ring. Ten times. Twenty.

"Hello," Lonnie's voice barked into the phone.

"Lonnie," Alan sputtered, the name just slipping out of his mouth.

"Shit. Is this Alan?" A giggle away from the phone. "Alan, goddamn, I'm busy."

"...I saw..." The words dribbled out slowly. Alan tried to fight the foam in his brain.

"Look, I'll see you later," Lonnie said. More giggles and the line clicked dead.

Alan's fingers touched the picture. No one held Alan's arm – always the third wheel. The little frozen images of Lonnie and Melissa seemed to move; they started laughing and pointing at Alan. His lips went cold, and the jealousy swelled into a ball in his stomach. He felt the woman's fingers working inside his body, guiding him to the door. He grabbed the gun case and clomped down the stairs.

His mom wasn't home, and he quickly glanced at the note his mother left – "picking up candy for the trick-or-treaters tonight." The clock above the dining room table read 2:45. Lonnie would be at Melissa's. Alan slammed the door shut, tossed the gun in the back of his car, and climbed into the driver's seat.

He drove, and despite her physical absence, the woman whispered about the times Lonnie ditched him, nights where Mel's folks would be out and Lonnie would break plans. Alan squeezed the steering wheel and stared ahead. Rain started to pelt his windshield, so he flicked on the wipers and watched the black bars send streams of water dribbling down the sides of his car. The seed of jealousy spread roots; the woman whispered her words well.

Mel lived a short drive south of town, and Alan had been there before. A sleepy October rain, cold but gentle, fell steadily now. He turned the key, shut off the engine, and listened to the raindrops tap the windshield. His right hand slipped to the passenger seat, and he pulled the gun case across his lap. His motions were automatic, guided by the hypnotic whisper oozing through his body as he unzipped the case without looking and slid the black barrel of the shotgun from its padded home. Alan's hands shook as he snapped five shells into the gun's magazine.

Her voice spoke into his ear. "Yes, Alan. Bring them both."

Alan stepped into the rain and slammed his car door shut. His clothes drank the cold water, and he was quickly soaked as he strode toward Melissa's door, clutching the shotgun as if he was on a hunt. He quietly stepped onto the porch and moved to a window. Melissa's parents were gone as usual. They wouldn't be back for hours.

He peered through the window. The room was dark except for the television flicker. Melissa and Lonnie lay entwined with one another on the couch, apparently asleep in a post-coital stupor, their

101

clothes spread on the floor and a thin blanket partially covering their bodies.

"Yes, Alan." The voice scraped the back of his neck. "They don't need you." The gun was heavy in his hand. His body was damp and thick with gooseflesh from the cold. Alan's eyes welled and turned to fogged glass as tears tumbled down his cheeks. The picture from last year's senior prom – the three smiling friends – slipped into his memory. He looked at the gun and slowly shook his head.

Alan crumbled on the porch like a pile of wet rags. He watched her bleed out of the rain, a simple figure advancing through the mist. One of her long hands stretched out and touched his cheek. It felt like a wash of icy water. Alan turned his head slightly and met her black gaze.

"Come to me, Alan. I need to show you something. I need to help you understand."

The rain slackened, but not before leaving the countryside damp and muddy. Alan stood next to his car and looked across the field. The day was drawing to a close, and darkness always fell early on Halloween. He could barely make out the line of trees in the twilight, but they were there. Alan circled to the passenger door and pulled out his shotgun and started toward the graves. The terrain fought against him – the muddy ground sucked at his sneakers, but the hypnotic pull was stronger. He was still drawn by the woman's quiet power. By the time he made it to the thicket, his once white shoes were completely doused with brown earth.

He plunged into the trees and winced as tips of branches slapped against his face, leaving a few superficial scratches and drawing blood from one deeper gouge on his right cheek. Although he couldn't see much through the trees, the clearing seemed to glow slightly. The woman, now swathed in dark brown and midnight colors, stood next to the big stone, waiting for him.

"Alan," she reached for him with a long finger and brushed a small bead of blood from his skin. He shivered at her touch. "I'm sorry." She looked into his eyes and held both of her icy hands to his face.

Alan staggered, still lost in a trace of his trance, and moved away from the woman. "I couldn't do it..."

"I want you to meet my children, Alan. You can't imagine what it was like. I did what I could to keep them from death. I did something awful. It was old magic – black magic." She swept closer to him. "They're stuck, Alan, almost alive, almost dead. I can't hunt for them, not now. I'm too weak. We are all too weak after all these years...until you and your friend came to us." A trace of black burned across her face. "We need to feed, to grow strong again. We need help for the hunt until we grow strong."

Alan slumped to the damp ground and looked around at the trees surrounding the little clearing. Dark shapes flitted between the grey lines of wood – shadows that began to take shape. He brought the gun across his lap and tightened his grip on the stock. "I...can't do...it," Alan stammered, "not...Lonnie...Mel."

"I thought they would be a good place to start. Friends always taste...better. I like you. I thought you could help us."

Alan closed his eyes for a moment. When he looked again, the shapes moved into the clearing, slowly at first like a melting fog. They were children, or had been children long ago. Now, they moved as pale things with black pits for eyes. Their movements were stiff, awkward, stretching and lurching after many motionless years. As they came closer to Alan, the thick, pungent smell of mud swelled, almost overwhelming him and driving him into the ground. The children were covered with the filth, and he noticed smudges on their pale faces. In a moment of panic, he pointed the gun at the nearest child, and it hissed, baring a black mouth full of jagged yellow teeth. Alan's finger quivered next to the trigger, but then he dropped the gun.

"You need to meet my children, Alan."

The whole mass, ten of them, pressed in around him, glaring with black, empty eyes. The smallest, only an infant, groped along the ground on hands and knees. One of the larger children tried to smile but just smashed its face into a hideous grimace. They were close enough that Alan felt their cold, damp breath and smelled the heavy scent of decay. One drew close to his leg, and tugged on his jeans, looking at Alan pathetically with those wide eyes.

The woman slipped next to him, whispering in his ear. "You can't let them go hungry, can you? Look at them." Her voice spun around his head like a cloud of thin smoke. He felt dizzy. "You can't let them go hungry, Alan. If you aren't ready to bring us your friend, start small."

The sky sunk into a deep blue with half of a moon throwing silver into the small clearing. "Yeah. Start small," Alan muttered before he grabbed his gun and stood. He moved in a trance again, guided by the woman and the bleary eyes of her children. His voice drifted from his mouth like a single note on a broken record. "Start small," he mumbled as he walked into the trees, remembering that it was Halloween night, and the streets would be filled with trick-or-treating children – an easy hunt indeed.

Dead Parachutes
by Catherine J. Gardner

The shopping cart screeched and whined its way down the road, heading one moment west, and the next taking a detour to the east to check out a gaggle of garbage cans. It seemed to have a purpose (other than to carry groceries), and if Dorothy Buchbander were of a mind to name the cart, she would have to call it Fred.

Dressed in a purple flannel robe, at two-thirty on a humid night in October, Dorothy stomped her foot and halted the cart in its tracks. A receipt flapped from the paper bags, addressed to a certain Jack Beard. Cans of tuna fish, carrots, eggplant and orange-flavored candy overflowed. Her middle finger tap tap tapped the front of the cart.

"If you're going to steal a fellow's groceries, at least have the decency to be quick about it," an Irish accent squawked.

Were Dorothy of a nervous disposition, the voice would have startled her.

Dorothy looked down as a garden gnome stepped onto her slippers. With sunken cheekbones, wizened eyes, and a shiny ring on his stubby thumb, there was nothing common or suburban about him.

"Excuse me, Missus, but aren't you a little past your retirement to be out this late on a Halloween morning?" he asked, scratching his grey beard. "Or is it a little early?"

Dorothy had half a mind to flick the plaster-mouthed thing up into the nearest tree. The nearest tree, however, stood in the front yard of her white clapboard house, and the damn thing would probably holler all night and give her no peace.

The fellow called Jack Beard jumped off her slipper and grasped hold of the cart. Unfortunately, it tipped forward and spilled both Jack and his groceries.

A dozen steak knives glinted in the moonlight as they stabbed down into the blacktop and speared both eggplant and Dorothy's toes.

Jack leapt to his feet and began gathering the knives, which, when clutched to his chest, proved as tall, or rather as small, as him. He grinned up at Dorothy in a way only a psychotic garden gnome can, and hurled one of them toward her face.

Luckily, Dorothy was prepared, and she flicked the knife to the left. The blade grazed her hand and clattered to the asphalt, awakening a light in the neighboring house.

A second knife whizzed through the air and nicked her ear, but her liver-spotted hands caught the next one and she twirled it in her fingers, pointing it toward the gnome.

"Your mother, or plaster cast, whatever the case may be," she growled, "should have told you not to mess with things bigger and uglier than you."

The cart, a definite Fred, squeaked in a backwards roll and then hurled itself down the road. It ended in a mangled heap as a juggernaut masquerading as an automobile careened into it and flipped it.

The next moment, a purple slipper stomped down on the head of the startled gnome. A crack ran from the tip of his red hat down his sharp nose and split him in two. Plaster dust exploded on the sidewalk.

Dorothy retrieved the cans of tuna fish and headed back into her clapboard house with its mimosa trees and clipped lawn, and made herself a midnight snack. She marked an X on the calendar, over October 30th. She had no cause to celebrate Halloween, but if it defecated on her doorstep, she would kick its hide and bury it deep in Providence Mount.

The scent of cats and urine usually warded things off. Dorothy added a liberal spray to her front stoop and to the back yard. For good measure, she waved across the road to the Del Grandes with a traditional, cantankerous old-woman single finger salute.

Albert Del Grande's hand stopped mid-wave and his wife's nose almost knocked a raven off the telephone wire, it turned up so high. They proceeded to climb into their 1994 Buick Skylark and creep away at ten miles per hour.

An extra spray for good luck drew a tabby cat across the yard and it headed up onto the stoop.

Jeez, first knife-wielding gnomes and now horny cats. Suburbia sure had its drawbacks.

The door quaked against its hinges as Dorothy slammed it shut. A crack ran down the stained glass.

She cracked her knuckles, ignored the cat pawing at her door, and settled down to some gentle old-dear rest and recuperation. As the chair rocked against the floorboards, Dorothy had to admit the patchwork quilt covering her knees was overkill. In addition, whatever she was knitting looked fit for an octopus. She held up the green mishmash of wool – a de-limbed octopus with six tentacles – and tossed it to the floor.

The mewling of the cat increased in number and a quick glance through her parlor window revealed a triumvirate of felines and a squad of bums.

The mailman sidestepped the invasion and whistled his way to the front door. He knocked with a cheery rappity-rap, and she figured he kicked his heels and performed a two-step whilst he waited.

Evil comes in many forms, and in many disguises, she thought.

The man's smile engaged. "Parcel for you madam."

Dorothy yanked the brown package out of his hands and signed the receipt with an illegible scrawl that was more insult than name.

"And will madam be attending the Plastic Surgery convention? He asked. "You know the drill. A few nips, the odd tug?"

Dorothy didn't get a chance to respond. A bum hobbled up the steps and sniffed first the mailman and second Dorothy.

Instead of plain old retiring, Dorothy considered changing teams and fighting on the side of all things bad. Had she a knitting needle at hand, she would have sealed the deal twofold.

"I'd send Mr. Buchbander to the car wash for a spruce up," the mailman said. And with that, the he snatched up his receipt, gave a bow and left.

Homicidal garden gnomes, a collection of horny cats and bums, and a want of decapitated mailmen. Dorothy let out a sigh. The world just kept giving. Welcome to Providence Mount, a nice place to live.

With the second slam of the door, the crack in the stained glass came close to shattering.

There was no tick to the parcel or hint of carnivorous mice, so she opened it. A Dot in the Box jumped out and laughed maniacally. That is, the Jack of tradition was fashioned like a mini Dorothy in her hey-day, complete with a purple jumpsuit spattered with yellow polka dots. It was a decade too late to admit it was not a good look.

"Enough already," she barked, and placed the thing down on the side table so that she could pull her granny pants out of her generous butt.

So much for incognito, going quiet into the long goodnight, etc, etc.

Suddenly, the world faded away in a brilliant flash that brought down ceiling and walls. Dorothy Buchbander stood in a dull shade of grey. She spat out plaster dust and picked pieces of glass out of her shock of white hair. Only the coiled spring of the mini Dot remained as it pinged and wobbled in the ruin of her home. Her fried cat clung, stupefied, to the banister.

The Del Grandes Buick Skylark screeched to a halt and Dorothy turned. Angela Del Grande's crows nest stood on end as she poked her beak out of the car window. Albert climbed out of the car and scratched his baldhead.

"Say neighbor," he called out, "is everything fine and dandy?"

Dorothy wiped a layer of soot off her purple pants and tucked in her yellow sweater. Her middle finger felt the urge to answer, but this was neither the time nor the situation. She waved her hand in an everything's a-okay gesture and sat down in her rocker, which – despite the explosion – continued to rock. However, it now rocked in the front yard.

Dorothy looked up at the ruin of her home.

Providence Mount: if we don't want you to stay, we won't be subtle in our eviction.

Angela Del Grande let out an effeminate eek as she stepped out of the car, and nearly tripped over a flambéed dead guy who now wore a hairpiece that strangely resembled a skinned cat. She kicked at it, and upon confirmation that the flesh was indeed cooked and breath baked, regained her composure.

"Something will have to be done about that eyesore," she said to her husband. "It can't rock there all day long."

Albert hushed his wife.

"I'm sure something of a murderous inclination will be along any moment," Dorothy said as she sat in her favorite chair. "Won't be more than a half-hour, I'm certain. Hurry along now. You have things to do I'm sure."

"Well, we were supposed to be at the convention for Plastic Surgeons this afternoon," Albert hesitated, "only…"

"Only?"

"Well, their practices proved a tad unorthodox."

"Unorthodox?"

Dorothy bit her lip. It tasted as if, rather than lipstick, she had applied some sort of *parrot* spell. She shook her head and rocked all the harder.

"They're plain cutting off people's bits…" Albert continued.

"Bits? Sorry, I shouldn't interrupt or we'll never be done."

"Not their bits *bits*," he insisted. "They wanted to saw off Angela's nose and replace it with plastic."

"Blue," Angela said, clasping her nose protectively. "I mean, who wants a sky-blue transparent nose?"

"That should just about do it," Dorothy said.

"Do what?" the Del Grandes asked.

"Move me, if not my rocker," Dorothy scowled.

The Buick proved a slow ride. Dorothy could have crawled faster, but the Del Grandes insisted and, well, she was going to need a place to stay for a day or so.

"Funny place for a convention, isn't it?" Angela said.

"No."

Dorothy surveyed the scene with indifference. Tents were set up in the forecourt of the Ravenous Motel, as if the fair had come to town. Or rather, a government who expected a riot, for the tents were neither gay, gaudy nor interesting.

A scream issued loud and long, and ended with a jet of blood spattering against a white canvas. A moment later, a pale hand rapped at the Buick's window and startled almost all of its occupants.

Dorothy, however, maintained her composure. She wound down her window and addressed the man in the surgical mask. "Alien, robot or evil human?"

"Plastic Surgeon."

That didn't really answer her question. In fact, it didn't answer it at all, but she accepted it anyway. She opened the Buick's door, and let the handle catch the surgeon in the crotch. The man's face contorted as he fell, proving at least that his anatomy was human-based.

"Excuse me," he squeaked.

"You're excused," Dorothy grumbled. She stepped over his crumpled body.

"Did you see that?" Angela Del Grande pecked, referring to the bloody canvas, not the debilitated surgeon. "Did you see that?"

Dorothy waddled over to the tents. A transparent blue arm lay on a pasting table in front of one, and she picked it up. The arm flexed, as if wanting her to feel its muscles, and she did so, but remained unimpressed. She used it to tap on the tent.

A head poked out.

"Yes."

"No."

"What?" A man stepped out of the tent. He had blood wiped down his otherwise gray laboratory coat.

"What if I was looking to invest in reconstructive surgery?" Dorothy inquired.

"It would cost your house, your auto and your pets," the man answered.

Dorothy looked towards the Buick. "I don't have a house, they're my neighbors, and that's not my car."

That seemed to do the trick. The felled plastic surgeon crawled away and disappeared inside his tent.

The day darkened.

Dorothy looked up. A chug, sputter, thump, thump, bang shuddered above her.

Albert wound down the Buick's window and braved the air. A tail of smoke followed in the wake of a nose-diving airplane.

"Incoming," the injured plastic surgeon shrieked as he dove under the pasting table.

Dorothy scratched her chin. Things were falling from the plane. Not things as in metal or glass, or flaming bits of the pilot and his crew. No. These things were parachutes.

A pink stiletto heel hurled kamikaze-like from the sky and stabbed into the Buick's roof, piercing the metal. Angela and Albert tumbled from the Buick in fear and assumed the fetal position.

Dorothy Buchbander had witnessed many vile, horrid things in her forty-year career, but never something so bizarre. Her eyes widened as she watched a flailing Dolly Parton fall from the plane. But there was more than one. Today there were at least eight of them. And they were already dead.

"Somebody save them," Albert cried.

"Somebody save us," Angela corrected.

"Amen," Dorothy muttered. She waggled her butt to free her underwear from her economy-sized crack.

Throwing the blue arm to the ground - where it proceeded to throttle the surgeon - Dorothy headed towards the road and the army of paratrooping Dollys.

The world shifted as the plane hit the ground.

Angela Del Grande crawled back into the Buick, beside her stupefied husband.

When the first Dolly landed, her feet sunk firmly into the ground, leaving holes in the blacktop. Her wig had slipped forward during the jump, and now covered one eye. The badge pinned to her prosthetic chest read: *Dollywood or bust!*

Dorothy tugged at her earlobe.

Of all the Dollys, in all of Province Mount.

"Nice day," she said.

"Nine to … nine to five," the disheveled Dolly stuttered, slamming the heel of her palm into her chin to correct her broken jaw.

"Well strictly, I work twenty-four seven, but yep. As it is only two-fifteen, I guess we are still in the average working day."

The six-foot, truck-wide dead Dolly lumbered forward unsteady on her heels. To her right, a more diminutive, wasp-waisted Dolly landed. Again, the same *Dollywood or bust!* pin blazed yellow on her chest. They looked at each other. They looked at Dorothy. They looked at the Del Grandes.

"There's no meat on my bones," Angela Del Grande said. "I was just explaining that to Albert. Albert, wasn't I just explaining how ..."

Fortunately, she didn't have enough time to finish her sentence. A giant, Hulk-Hoganesque Dolly landed behind her and picked her up by her beak.

Angela's legs shook as she dangled six inches off the ground. She didn't stay there for long, though. A moment later, Dolly Hogan's arm lit up like a roman candle on the Fourth of July.

Apparently they weren't invincible to the flesh-burning Tennessee sunlight.

Dorothy watched the intriguing turn of events from a distance. Dead Dollys, it seemed, were not as stupid as Dead Handymen or Dead Wal-Mart employees - two previous zombie threats. They bustled on past her and headed into the tents, away from the angry Tennessee sun.

Dorothy rubbed her hands together. "Well that's that, I suppose."

"What do you mean? They're ... they're ..." Angela's fingers stabbed toward the tent. "In there."

"Oh, they won't come out again until sundown," Dorothy assured her.

However, that wasn't the end of the excitement. A scream surged up the road and up sprinted a flaming Dolly.

Albert Del Grande doubled up in horror and as the undead woman screamed past. But this one didn't make it into the tent. The flaming Dolly stopped dead in her tracks and toppled over, just outside the canvas flap.

Dorothy smiled. A prosthetic arm to the temple did the trick nicely. The zombie's decapitated head, sans wig, rolled down the road and under a yellow school bus, which promptly squished it.

The driver saluted Dorothy as he passed.

Now Dorothy was starting to like this town. It wasn't as boring as she thought. Perhaps she would rebuild and stick around after all.

The school bus took out two more Dead Dollys as they headed towards a Wendy's Hamburger joint, and Dorothy couldn't help but smile.

If she'd used a vehicle like that, perhaps she would have made it into the pages of DC or Marvel. The costume certainly hadn't worked. Nor had the artists' impressions she'd sent of Dizzy Dot.

Why deal in fact when you can peddle fiction?

The yellow bus headed back towards the motel forecourt.

"Hey," Angela Del Grande exclaimed, fingers stabbing, "I know him! That's not the bus driver."

"Guilty as charged," the driver said as he hopped off the bus. "Eduardo Lichtzer, at your service. Well, that's not my real name, but…"

Dorothy hiked up her sweats. "Excuse me," she said, stepping past the uppity newcomer.

Behind the tent, a de-wigged Dolly had taken a bite from a Dolly dangling from a lamppost. Dorothy interrupted the dead girl's meal by twisting her head off with a yank, and stomping on her chest for good measure.

The Dolly's skin felt dry. The innards, however, glistened wet, red, and raw.

The dangling Dolly began to flame.

"Sorry about that," Dorothy addressed the de-wigged, de-headed Dolly. "I'm sure you love a good barbecue."

"Excuse me. Do you have a biographer?" Eduardo inquired, approaching the elderly superhero. "Because I'm chief editor of *The Surreal Papers*, and yours is a fascinating story."

"Comic book, graphic novel?"

"Written word, but we do have a dandy fellow who draws a monthly cartoon about a lonely bat."

Dorothy growled, and the zombie-filled tent shuffled about ten paces in retreat. She didn't like the sound of that.

Meanwhile, a fire-truck sped down the road, heading toward the ruined plane. Smoke plumed in the distance, and a white SUV full of plastic surgeons sped in the opposite direction.

They'd had quite enough of the undead Dolly Partons.

"Sometimes it's hard to be a woman," Tammy Wynette sang, as undead Dolly-Hogan was pushed from the tent. She tried to stand up, but the sun was simply too hot. She exploded, sending rags of skin over telephone wires, and leaving stiletto heels on the forecourt.

"I told you I hate Halloween," Angela Del Grande cursed. She wobbled forward unsteadily, as if both heels and brain had snapped simultaneously, and fell heavily against the pasting table. Her crow's nest was ruined and mascara ran down her cheeks.

"I absolutely *hate* it!"

Author Bios

Christopher Fulbright is the author of the recent horror story collection 'WHEN IT RAINS' AND OTHER WRECKAGE (Doorways Publications, 2007), and co-author of the novellas THEN COMES THE CHILD (Carnifex Press, 2006) and BLOOD COVEN (Dead Letter Press, 2007), written with his wife Angeline Hawkes. He's also the author of numerous short stories, the most recent of which are scheduled to appear in the upcoming anthologies BOOK OF DEAD THINGS (Twilight Tales), ELDRITCH STEEL (Elder Signs Press) and BOUND FOR EVIL (Dead Letter Press). Some magazines his stories have appeared in include The Book of Dark Wisdom, Outer Darkness, Haunts, Peep Show, and Thirteen Stories, with honorable mentions in The Year's Best Fantasy and Horror 2006, and the Writers of the Future contest in 2007.

Rob Rosen is the author of the critically acclaimed novel, *Sparkle*. His short stories have appeared, to date, in more than fifty anthologies. Please visit him at his website, www.therobrosen.com, or email him at robrosen@therobrosen.com.

Lawrence Dagstine has been writing dark, pulpy tales of science fiction, fantasy, and horror since 1996. His short fiction has graced *many* a paying, print, and online venue within the genre field. Over 310+ publication credits in twelve years, but he still calls it his little side hobby. Sam's Dot Publishing is releasing his first collection in late 2008-early 2009. Considered by friends a die-hard scifi geek and horror fanatic, he comes from Brooklyn, New York, where he lives with his beautiful wife and son, dreaming the great writer's dream .... Visit his website at: www.lawrencedagstine.com.

Tom Johnstone is a municipal gardener by trade. So he spends his days carrying out park functions, and his nights carrion out dark fictions - published in *Midnight Horror*, *Dark Tales* and *Dark Fire Tales...*

Karen L. Newman has been a published writer since 2004 in the horror, science fiction and fantasy genres and is an active member of Horror Writers Association. Over two hundred and fifty of her short stories and poems have been published both online and in print. Her story credits include *Cthulhu Sex* (upcoming), *Nocturnal Ooze*, *Aoife's Kiss*, *7th Dimension*, and *Sinister Tales*. Her poetry collections include *EEKU* (Sam's Dot, 2005), *ChemICKals* (Naked Snake Press, 2007), and *Toward Absolute Zero* (Sam's Dot, 2009). Her work has been nominated for a Rhysling Dwarf Star Award. She won the 2005 Mary Jane Barnes Award and two of her poems received honorable mention in *The Year's Best Fantasy and Horror*. She lives in Kentucky where she edits the online magazine *Afterburn SF*, which publishes speculative short stories, and is the editor for the print poetry magazine *Illumen*. She also writes reviews for *Dark Discoveries*. Please visit her online at http://home.zoomnet.net/~karennew.

Christopher Allan Death currently resides in the concrete jungle of Northern Colorado. He has published fiction in Worlds of Wonder, Night to Dawn, The Ethereal Gazette, 7th Dimension Magazine, and Bits of the Dead (Coscom Entertainment), among others. His novella, *Welcome to Wonderland*, will soon be published by Lyrical Press, Inc.

Sam Leng has had fiction published in a number of magazines, including Sinister Tales, Twisted Tongue, Theaker's Quarterly Fiction, Skive Magazine, and more. She produces her own fiction and poetry magazine, which can be found online at www.neonbeam.org. She lives in Yorkshire, England, with Worzel Gummidge and a biscuit barrel.

Since 2006 **Kris Ashton** has published more than a dozen stories and is fast making a name for himself as one of Australia's hottest speculative fiction writers. His first novel, *Ghost Kiss*, is now available through US publisher Asylett Press. He lives in Sydney with his fiancé and their two boxer dogs.

Aaron Polson is a high school English teacher who dreams in black and white with Rod Serling narration. When he isn't arguing about the definition of irony with his students, he can be found chipping away at some twisted tale. He currently resides in Lawrence, Kansas with his wife and two sons. His short fiction has appeared in various places, including Reflection's Edge, GlassFire Magazine, Big Pulp, Johnny America, and Permuted Press's Monstrous anthology. You can visit him on the web at www.frozenrobot.com.

Catherine J Gardner's fiction has appeared in over sixty magazines, anthologies and online. She has work forthcoming in The Age of Blood & Snow anthology, Sand and Twisted Dreams. You can find her online at http://fright-fest.blogspot.com.

Steve Cartwright has done art for several magazines, newspapers, websites, commercial and governmental clients, books, and scribbling – but mostly drooling – on tavern napkins. He has also created art pro bono for several animal rescue groups. He was awarded the 2004 James Award for his cover art for Champagne Shivers. He recently illustrated the Cimarron Review and Stories for Children covers. Take a gander (or a goose) at his online gallery: www.angelfire.com/sc2/cartoonsbycartwright.

www.ingramcontent.com/pod-product-compliance
Lightning Source LLC
Chambersburg PA
CBHW030635130626
46552CB00002B/870